A Candlelight Ecstasy Romance®

"TONI! I THOUGHT YOU MIGHT DROP BY. . . ."

Before he could finish the sentence, she marched to his desk, picked up the vase of fresh flowers, and poured it over his head.

Reaching into his back pocket for a clean handkerchief, he calmly mopped at the stream of water dripping in rivulets down his face. "I know you would rather die than let me know it, but you're upset about something, aren't you?"

"You know perfectly well what I'm upset about—you dirty rat!"

"Now hold on a minute. Jim called me last night and told me what happened, and I want to apologize to you—"

"Save your breath. I don't appreciate your implying to your friends that I'm a loony tune, Mr. Tremayne, so just stop it! And don't even talk to me. Not ever again!" She whirled around, went out the door, then slammed it with a resounding bang.

CANDLELIGHT ECSTASY CLASSIC ROMANCES

CANDLELIGHT ECSTASY ROMANCES®

QUANTITY SALES

Most Dell Books are available at special quantity discounts when purchased in bulk by corporations, organizations, and special-interest groups. Custom imprinting or excerpting can also be done to fit special needs. For details write: Dell Publishing Co., Inc., 1 Dag Hammarskjold Plaza, New York, NY 10017, Attn.: Special Sales Dept., or phone: (212) 605-3319.

INDIVIDUAL SALES

Are there any Dell Books you want but cannot find in your local stores? If so, you can order them directly from us. You can get any Dell book in print. Simply include the book's title, author, and ISBN number, if you have it, along with a check or money order (no cash can be accepted) for the full retail price plus 75¢ per copy to cover shipping and handling. Mail to: Dell Readers Service, Dept. FM, P.O. Box 1000, Pine Brook, NJ 07058.

OUT OF THIS WORLD

Lori Copeland

A CANDLELIGHT ECSTASY ROMANCE®

Published by
Dell Publishing Co., Inc.
1 Dag Hammarskjold Plaza
New York, New York 10017

Dell ® TM 681510, Dell Publishing Co., Inc.

Candlelight Ecstasy Romance®, 1,203,540, is a registered trademark of Dell Publishing Co., Inc., New York, New York.

ISBN: 0-440-16764-7

Printed in the United States of America

October 1986

10 9 8 7 6 5 4 3 2 1

WFH

*To the girls on my Monday night bowling
team:*

*Annavee Duncan, Jan Burlison,
Billie Murdock,
Jocelyn Klein, Mona Gillihan, and
Kay McClelland.*

To Our Readers:

We have been delighted with your enthusiastic response to Candlelight Ecstasy Romances®, and we thank you for the interest you have shown in this exciting series.

In the upcoming months we will continue to present the distinctive sensuous love stories you have come to expect only from Ecstasy. We look forward to bringing you many more books from your favorite authors and also the very finest work from new authors of contemporary romantic fiction.

As always, we are striving to present the unique, absorbing love stories that you enjoy most—books that are more than ordinary romance. Your suggestions and comments are always welcome. Please write to us at the address below.

Sincerely,

The Editors
Candlelight Romances
1 Dag Hammarskjold Plaza
New York, New York 10017

CHAPTER ONE

A small economy car pulling a U-Haul trailer turned down Fallow Drive and slowed to a crawling pace. The large elm trees shading the street were a pleasant and welcome sight to the young woman who had driven nearly nonstop for the last twenty-four hours to reach her destination.

Her eyes scanned the street numbers intently as the car crept along. The houses on Fallow Drive were at least twenty years old, their lawns boasting neatly tended flowerbeds and well-trimmed shrubbery. Massive old trees lined the sheltered street, their boughs nearly touching each other and forming a canopy of green.

Toni Cameron drew in a long, cleansing breath of the perfumed May air. In another few weeks, people had told her, Texas would be dry and almost unbearably hot, but for today it looked like sheer heaven to her.

Forty-seven sixteen. This was it.

Braking carefully, she pulled alongside the curb and brought the car to a halt. Her eyes surveyed the homey-looking vine-covered cottage before her, and she heaved a sigh of relief.

The rental agency had assured her that the duplex she had rented sight unseen would be suitable for her needs, but she had worried all the way from Iowa that she had made a mistake. But now, without even seeing the inside, she knew it was right.

Restarting the engine, she pulled forward until the end of the trailer had cleared the drive and then stopped again. Backing trailers was not exactly her area of expertise, but at the moment she had no other choice than to attempt the feat.

Slipping the transmission into reverse, she closed her eyes, prayed for skills she knew she didn't have the slightest hope of possessing, took another deep breath, and then began.

She had no idea how she accomplished it, but within twenty seconds the trailer was sideways in the drive and the car was butted straight up against it. Shaking her head disgustedly, she put the car into low gear and pulled forward again.

This time she didn't make it ten feet before the trailer wheel hit the curb, throwing her head forward and bringing her to a jolting, abrupt halt.

Rubbing her neck painfully, she grimaced and jerked the car back into forward. The trailer thumped loudly over the curb and left a black streak of rubber as it shot back out onto the street.

She knew that every dish she owned had just been wiped out, but what could she do?

Grumbling irritably under her breath, she yanked the car back into reverse and gunned the trailer back over the curb, leaving a trail of blue smoke as it bounced up in the air and landed in the middle of one of the tidy, manicured flower beds that lined the twin drives.

And there went all her other fragile objects, including the glass refrigerator shelves! she thought impatiently.

Zackery Tremayne glanced up from washing his car and watched the dirt and pieces of rosebushes spewing up in the air with amazement as the wheels of the trailer tried to dig their way out of one of *his* flower beds.

Once more the squeal of rubber filled the air as the trailer shot back out onto the pavement and came to a screeching halt.

Woman drivers! He shook his head in amusement and turned his attention back to what he had been doing.

But a few minutes later, it became hard to ignore the sound of bushes being snapped off and ground under the tires of her car as she once more made a wild stab at getting the trailer backed into her drive.

Grumbling good-naturedly under his breath, he pitched the soapy sponge into a bucket of water, then jumped the small hedge that separated the two drives and walked over to where she was sitting still, now with the motor idling.

"Hi."

Toni had been so lost in thought as to what she was going to do next that the sound of his voice startled her.

"Sorry," he apologized, noting the way she had nearly jumped out of her skin. "I didn't mean to scare you, but I thought you could use some help." His gaze discreetly surveyed the car, which was now

11

jackknifed around the trailer, and then came back to her as he stuck out his hand in a friendly greeting. "Zack Tremayne. You must be my new neighbor?"

"Hi. Toni Cameron, and yes, I sure could use some help," she accepted gratefully as she slid out of the driver's seat and turned to face him. "I'm afraid I'm not very good at backing trailers."

He was bare-chested, barefooted, and wearing a pair of white tennis shorts, but he looked like a six-foot-one, hazel-eyed angel of mercy to her.

"They're tricky," he admitted, and flashed her a winning smile if she had ever seen one. "I'll be glad to do it for you."

Sliding behind the wheel of the car, he eased it forward, and within a few minutes he had the car gliding smoothly up the tree-lined drive.

Toni stood back and shook her head in awe, envying the ease with which he handled the car. Eventually she would have managed to get the trailer where she wanted it, but she shuddered to think how long it would have taken her.

While the task was being finished, her gaze unthinkingly focused on the handsome white knight driving her car. She certainly couldn't have asked for a more attractive liberator.

He was at least a head taller than she was, and his hair was brown—no, actually, it was more of a dark blond—and it had a little bit of natural curl to it, which gave it a look of controlled disorder that Toni had always found appealing. He had a nice tan that set off his eyes, which were a most attractive and unusual shade of green, and she had noticed a deep

12

dimple on his left cheek when he grinned at her. And it certainly wasn't hard to see that he was in fine physical shape. He wasn't muscle-bound, but he had that nice firm look about him that bespoke masculine strength and power.

One of those real heartbreakers, she thought absently, the sort of man she planned to avoid from now on.

By now he had the trailer backed neatly to the side porch and was getting out of the car. "There, that ought to fix you up." He smiled. "The trick is turning the wheel in the opposite direction you want the trailer to go."

"I can't thank you enough." She smiled, then frowned apologetically. "I hope I haven't done too much damage to the neighborhood—and your flower bed."

He smiled back. "I don't think so. You new to the area?"

"Yes, I just drove here from Des Moines."

"Des Moines, huh? What brings you such a long way from home? Your husband get transferred to Texas or something?" With male appreciation, his gaze ran lightly over the attractive blonde standing before him.

She wasn't very tall, but she was definitely well built. His eyes were reluctant to move away from the snug-fitting T-shirt she was wearing, although he was careful to maintain a polite decorum while he looked. Her hair was long and the rich color of honey, but she had chosen to pull it away from her face into a ponytail; somehow, the carefree style made her look much younger than he guessed her to

13

be. She had laughing blue eyes, a perky little nose that tilted ever so slightly when she grinned, and a most sensational pair of legs.

He could have done a whole lot worse in a new neighbor, he quickly decided, forcing his gaze to safer territory.

"No, I'm not married," she corrected. Funny how that thought still seemed to rankle her, even now. "I just decided I needed a change of scenery."

"Well, I hope Texas treats you well." He stuck out his hand once more and shook hers. "Let me know if I can be of any further help."

"I will, and thanks again, Mr. Tremayne. I'll get that flower bed back in order as soon as possible."

"Hey, I promise I won't call you Ms. Cameron if you won't call me Mr. Tremayne. Let's make it Zack and Toni." He grinned again and jumped the hedge to his side of the drive.

"That sounds fair to me, Zack." She watched as he walked back to his shiny red Mazda RX-7 and went back to work.

Turning her attention back to the enormous job of unloading the trailer, she found herself unwilling to face the task as total fatigue closed in on her. Perhaps she would go inside and explore her new home and rest a few minutes before she tackled the awesome job.

The duplex, with its shiny new coat of fresh white paint, had a side entrance, and she quickly decided this would be the door she would be using the most often. Stepping up the three concrete steps that led to the side porch, she inhaled deeply and delighted in the smell of the dark crimson roses that were

14

climbing up a large trellis beside the door. Their sweet perfume floated lightly on the air as she unlocked the door and stepped into the cool interior of the living room.

It was only a three-room house, but the rooms were large and airy, and they looked very comfortable. There was a set of French doors off the living room, and the realtor had told her they led to a small backyard.

She wandered over to the doors and opened them, then walked out into the afternoon sunshine. Like the front of the house, the backyard was shady and inviting. There was even a tiny patch of dirt sitting over in the corner where the sun peeked through. It looked as if someone had once had a garden there.

Tomato plants and pole beans, she quickly decided. That's what she would plant. And she could watch them grow and produce and then harvest their bounty all summer long.

She stood in the lush, freshly mown grass a few more moments savoring the warm rays of sunlight on her face before she finally turned and went back into the house.

The bedroom proved to be the smallest room in the house, but it was more than adequate for what little furniture she had brought with her. It had a lovely covered window seat where she could sit and look outside. She would like that. The house she had lived in before had very few windows, and she had missed the outside light.

In view of the fact she had only a bed, a sofa, a portable television, two end tables, one lamp, a refrigerator, a card table, and two kitchen chairs, she really didn't need a lot of space. It wasn't very much to show for a woman who would soon be thirty-one years old, but she consoled herself with the thought that she was still young and could start over again.

Only this time, she would be more careful.

The kitchen was cheerful, even though it, too, was compact. There was a large window overlooking the driveway that would provide a cool breeze and a pleasant view. Coupled with the fact that she would only be twenty minutes away from the county courthouse, where she would start her new job as a court stenographer first thing in the morning, the house was more than suitable for her needs.

Now her only problem was to get the trailer unloaded and back to the rental agency before she had to pay another day's fee. She knew she could manage everything but the sofa and refrigerator herself; those two heavy items would present her biggest challenge. Friends had helped her load them onto the trailer in Des Moines, but she didn't have those friends to help her now.

An hour later, she was still wondering what she would do as she set the last box on the card table in the kitchen and looked around her. She was all finished, except for the two heavy items remaining on the trailer.

A soft rap on the side door interrupted her musings; she dusted off her hands and went to see who it was.

"Hi, again." Zack Tremayne stood on the small porch and smiled politely at her. He was now dressed in a pair of dress slacks and a sport shirt, and he looked much more presentable than he had

16

earlier. Even this early in the season, he had a dark tan and a healthy look about him that most men would envy. The gentle breeze that drifted by him caught the very pleasant scent of his soap and after-shave.

Toni found herself extremely happy to see him again. Brushing absently at a stray wisp of honey-brown hair, she opened the door wider. "Hi there. What brings you over the wall again?" she said teasingly.

He chuckled. "I've been watching you unload that trailer for the last hour, and although you've done an amazing job of wrestling those boxes around by yourself, I honestly don't see how you're going to manage that refrigerator and sofa."

She laughed at his astute assessment of her latest predicament. "Would you believe I don't know how I'm going to, either?"

"Then you wouldn't object to my offering my help once again?"

She looked at him thoughtfully. "Are you sure you really want to? You look as if you have more important things to do than help me move." He looked spit-shined and polished, and every stylish dark blond hair was in place. She knew a man as good-looking as he was must undoubtedly be antici-pating a more stimulating evening than moving fur-niture.

"I have a few minutes before I have to keep an appointment," he assured her.

"Well, if you're sure you have the time, then I'll admit I sure could use the help."

He stepped back as she opened the screen door

17

and slipped out to stand beside him. "I really do appreciate this," she chattered as they walked off the porch together. "I have to have the trailer back to the rental agency in another hour, and I hated the thought of having to try to hire someone to unload it in addition to having to pay another day's rent on it."

In a few minutes they were standing at the trailer, and even though there were two of them now, the chore of getting the refrigerator unloaded still seemed monumental to her.

"I don't know—what do you think?" She looked up at him hopefully.

"Looks pretty heavy," he conceded.

"You think we can handle it ourselves?"

"Nope."

"No?"

"No, that's why just before I came over I took the liberty of calling a good friend to come over and give me a hand," he confessed. His eyes traveled over the tan shorts and red T-shirt that he had admired earlier. Red had always been his favorite color, but she made it even more appealing. "Your muscles are much prettier than Jim's, but I'm afraid his are more suited to moving refrigerators than yours are."

Toni let out a sigh of relief. "Thanks again. I don't know if my back would have held out or not."

Seconds later, a bright red Pontiac Fiero pulled up in front of Zack's house, and the driver tooted its horn playfully.

Placing the tips of his fingers in the corners of his

18

mouth, Zack let out an ear-piercing whistle. "Over here!"

Toni's ears were still ringing as the driver jumped out of his car and bounded over the hedge. "Hey! What's happenin', Tremayne?"

"Not much, Howerton. You made good time."

"Yeah, traffic was pretty light." The new arrival looked at Toni, and his grin widened as he stuck out his hand in a friendly gesture. "And this must be the beautiful damsel in distress?"

"Toni Cameron, this is my good friend, Jim Howerton. Toni's my new neighbor," Zack explained.

"Lucky you." Jim punched Zack in the ribs knowingly, then shook her hand energetically. "Toni, nice to meet you."

"Hello, Jim. It's very nice to meet you, too."

"So this is what we have to unload." Jim's pleasant brown eyes surveyed the refrigerator and sofa thoughtfully. "No sweat. It shouldn't take us but a few minutes."

Toni stood back as Zack climbed into the trailer, slipped a dolly under the refrigerator, and strapped it down tightly. Within half an hour, the trailer had been unloaded and the articles neatly placed in their new positions.

"I can't thank you two enough," Toni said again as she walked back outside with them. "I don't know what I would have done without you."

"No trouble," Zack assured her.

"None at all," Jim seconded. "Say, I'll bet Toni hasn't eaten yet. Why don't we all go grab a sandwich somewhere?"

"Sounds like fun, but I have an appointment at

seven," Zack declined apologetically. "Maybe some other time."

"Oh? Well, I guess Toni and I could survive without you." Jim grinned at her. "What do you think? I know a great little Italian place that makes delicious meatball sandwiches."

Toni smiled ruefully. "That's very nice of you, but I'm afraid I can't make it, either. I still have to get the trailer to the rental agency, and then all I want to do is come home for a hot bath and a good night's rest. I haven't been to bed for close to thirty hours, and I'm exhausted."

She walked with the men to the hedge and paused to express her gratitude once again.

"Really, it was no trouble at all," Zack reiterated. "If anything else comes up that you can't handle, just raise your kitchen window and give me a holler."

"Thank you. I will."

"The same for me," Jim offered. "I'm in the phone book and not more than twenty minutes away."

"Thank you. I'll keep that in mind."

A few minutes later, Toni stood on the porch and watched Jim and Zack go off in their separate cars. She gave them both a friendly wave and watched their cars disappear down the street.

For a moment the ever-familiar feeling of loneliness washed over her as she thought about the fact that she was in a new town where she knew no one but the two men who had just driven away. And they were only very polite strangers.

The loneliness will get better, she reminded herself, but it wasn't the first time she had had to make an effort to believe it.

It simply had to.

A soft breeze sprang up and gently kissed her cheeks as she turned and walked back into her house. It was as if the breeze had decided to be her friend just when she felt she had none. The scent of roses still perfumed the air, and the massive old elms still shaded the tree-lined street; but somehow none of those things were as comforting to her as they had been a little earlier.

It was nearly nine o'clock by the time she returned the trailer to the rental agency and stopped at a fast-food chain for a hamburger and soft drink. On arriving home, she found the box with the bed linens and made her bed. That accomplished, she took her eagerly anticipated hot bath and slipped into a lightweight cotton gown.

A cooling breeze rustled through the leaves of the tree next to her bedroom window. She sat down on the corner of her bed and absently ran a brush through her hair. The sound of the leaves was particularly pleasant, since there had been no trees close to the house where she had lived before.

Strolling over to the window while she rubbed an almond-scented lotion onto her arms, she let her gaze absently wander to the shadowy yard beside the house. The house next door was dark and quiet. It was still early, and her new neighbor, Zack, had not returned from his "appointment" yet.

She had to smile when she thought about how nice he had been to her. Not everyone would have offered their help the way he had. And Jim wasn't bad, either.

Switching off the lamp beside her bed, she sat down on the window seat and gazed upward at the stars. The night was crystal clear, and she could see the Big Dipper stretching across the sky in a brilliant display of heavenly lights.

In a little game she had played ever since her father had taken her outside one starry night when she was just a small child and pointed out all the interesting things that were in the sky, her eyes began to search for the Milky Way, and then they traveled slowly across the diamond-lit sky to search for satellites orbiting the earth. If by chance she were able to locate one, then it would become a different game to try and guess if it was the United States' or Russia's. Someone had once told her there was a difference in the two superpowers' satellites, but no matter how hard she tried, she had never been able to distinguish between them.

She yawned and stretched as exhaustion threatened to overtake her now. The hot bath and the quiet moments were beginning to relax her. Casting one last glance toward the starry heavens, she slid off the window seat and stood up.

Suddenly, a bright object in the western sky caught her eye. Ever so slowly, she leaned closer to the window and sought to make out more clearly the tiny dot of glowing light that seemed to be picking up speed and traveling in her direction.

She stood for a moment and watched the strange light grow steadily brighter.

She climbed back up in the window sill and tried

to focus her sleepy gaze on the object. It was moving fast, still picking up speed and coming her way.

A plane, or some other kind of low-flying aircraft, she reasoned. That's all it was. Her shoulders drooped with relief. For a minute she had thought she might have spotted one of those UFO's that had stirred up such a controversy several years ago. She chuckled to herself at her wild imaginings and started to stand up once again, but something made her cast another quizzical glance out the window.

No, wait. No plane would be moving that fast, she realized. The object hurtling toward her was growing larger now, and its speed was hard to determine, but it was not a plane. She was sure of it.

Her eyes widened as the object came steadily closer and closer. As if in a daze, she slid off the window seat and crept through the darkened living room, pausing at each window to see if it was still there. Each time it was, only it seemed to grow larger by the minute.

Her breath came in short spurts as she opened the side door and slipped out onto the porch. The smooth concrete felt cool to her bare feet, and she realized that she had forgotten to put on her slippers, but it didn't matter. The glowing object was nearly over Zack's house now. As it approached, it paused, then cut back for a few minutes and hovered about a hundred feet off the ground. She guessed the craft to be about fifteen to twenty feet in diameter, and it had red, green, and yellow lights rotating around the rim.

Her heart was hammering so hard, she could feel it beating in her chest. She stepped over the low hedge and cautiously peeked around the corner of the house where the craft was now stationary directly over Zack's backyard.

She could hear no sound coming from the vessel; only the eerie flashing of lights told her it was there. The neighborhood dogs started barking, the only noise to break the uneasy silence that seemed to cloak the earth now.

As she huddled behind the house, a bright yellow beam shot out of one of the portholes of the saucer-shaped object and scanned the yard and the tops of the trees for a few minutes. It paused periodically on the lawn furniture, and then it suddenly turned around and focused an unusual amount of attention on Zack's odd-shaped barbecue grill.

After a few moments it traveled on slowly about the yard, then turned around abruptly once more and came back to the grill, pausing once again as the shaft from the light enlarged. Toni could see particles of dust swirling in the light, as if they were being suctioned up into the body of the ship, as the beam riveted on the grill and stayed there.

She was mesmerized by the strange object, and she couldn't tear her eyes away from the sight, although she was about to faint from fright. She could see the branches of a nearby tree swaying, and the light poles and wiring surrounding the house were aglow with a peculiar bluish light.

There was something about the grill that fascinated the object. Its lights continued to focus on the spindly red kettle until Toni decided it would never move on.

Five minutes later, its curiosity apparently satis-

24

fied for the moment, the beam of light swung back over the house. She hurriedly ducked her head back around the corner and held her breath until the ray disappeared back into the body of the craft moments later. Then, as suddenly as it had appeared, the thing shot upward in a rush of wind and back into the ebony sky.

Crawling on her hands and knees, she rounded the corner of the house and sat transfixed as she watched the glowing object move away from her at a speed that could not be comprehended, and grow smaller and smaller in the distant sky.

Reaching up to touch her face, she could feel the wetness sliding down her cheeks as the wind from the strange object still tossed her hair about in wild disarray. Numb, in a state of shock, she reached up to wipe away the tears of fright—or were they tears of wonder?—as her gaze continued to follow the ship until it completely disappeared into a black void.

Then an awesome quiet descended over the backyard.

It was several moments later before the tree frogs and cicadas started up again. The wind made a gentle rustling sound through the leaves of the trees as she sank weakly down onto the dew-covered grass and listened.

It was as if the last fifteen minutes had never taken place.

Rising to her feet slowly, her gaze still refused to leave the brilliant heavens, hoping for one last sign of the unexplainable object. But whatever it had been, it was there no longer. Only tiny diamonds twinkling back at her from a backdrop of black velvet met her gaze as she scanned the sky one final time.

Good heavens! Had she gone completely bananas, or had she just seen a flying saucer?

Her feet suddenly sprouted wings as she found herself racing back to the safety of her house. Surely an object that big would have been seen by other people. If so, then the police would have reports of it.

Her hands were shaking so hard, she could hardly find her car keys, but she finally did, then raced back out the front door. Since her phone was not in working order yet, she would have to go down to the one on the corner that she had seen earlier today to make a call.

Ten minutes later, she was standing outside her car, still dressed in her housecoat, her nerves strung tight as a fiddle's as she dialed the operator. There were several long, agonizing rings before a woman's voice came on the line.

"Operator."

"The police—give me the police station, please."

"One moment, pleeeeze."

A new series of rings began, promptly followed by a male voice. "Police Department."

"Yes—uh, my name's Toni Cameron, and I live on Fallow Drive."

"Yes."

"Yes, well, I was wondering—have you had any reports of a strange object being in this area tonight?" she prompted hopefully. "Say, in the last fifteen minutes?"

"Strange objects?"

"Yes, strange, glowing objects," she encouraged, "objects that sort of make the trees and the power lines look kind of—bluish." Even as she spoke the words, she knew how ridiculous they sounded.

"Bluish, huh? Just a minute, ma'am. I'll check."

Moments later he was back on the line. "No, ma'am. We haven't had any reports of bluish objects in your area."

"Oh, dear, you haven't?"

"No, ma'am. Are you wanting to make one?"

"Me? Oh, no thanks. I was just wondering."

She replaced the receiver on the hook, then immediately jerked it back off and punched the operator button again. *Surely* someone had seen what she had and reported it.

"Operator."

"I need the local newspaper office."

"One moment, please."

It took a few minutes to get through to the news desk, but the answer was the same. No such report had been turned in, but the reporter had laughingly asked her if she had seen a flying saucer, which she had promptly denied.

She had the same result when she called a couple of television and radio stations. Apparently she was the only one who had seen the strange object, and she wasn't about to admit to such an occurrence if no one else had seen it.

Casting one last exasperated look upward, she slid back into her car and started the engine.

If this had been the work of her imagination, then it certainly was up for an Academy Award this time.

CHAPTER TWO

The sound of birds singing in the trees awakened her the next morning. It was a comforting, normal sound, and she assured herself that it was okay to wake up and face the new day.

Had she actually seen a flying saucer, or had she only dreamed she had?

Rolling over onto her side, Toni forced her eyes open just as a new and beautiful dawn was breaking. Sunshine was streaming through the leaves of the tree outside the window, casting a pretty, symmetrical pattern across her bed.

She felt groggy and listless. As tired as she had been last night, she still had not slept well. Her mind kept reliving the incident that had taken place earlier, and, try as she might, she had not been able to relax and go to sleep until the early hours of the morning.

It had occurred to her that she might confide in her new neighbor what had taken place in his backyard, but she hadn't heard his car pull into the drive until close to two this morning. Besides, he would probably never believe her. And who in his right mind could blame him? Even she wasn't sure it had really happened.

Perhaps she had been more mentally exhausted than she had first thought. The last three weeks had been enough to test anyone's sanity.

Sliding out of bed, she reached for the light robe on the end of the bed and slipped it on.

Breaking up with Skip had taken a lot out of her. Not that she wouldn't eventually get over him, given enough time, and she thought she was doing pretty darn well, considering the traumatic experience. Coming out of a relationship she had nurtured and cherished for the past two years still fully intact was just one more thing to be thankful for.

Maybe she was still a wee bit shaky, but it was getting better all the time.

Oh, at first she had fallen apart. After all, she had spent the last two years of her life living with Skip Harden, always with the promise that marriage was in the near future for them. But it had never taken place, so she had finally made the inevitable break.

Now, after the initial shock of the separation had worn off, Toni was beginning to see that what had happened between them was probably for the best.

Even months before the breakup had actually occurred, she had toyed with the idea of severing the relationship. As far as she could see, they were getting no closer to the altar than they ever had been.

But somehow she hadn't found the strength to actually give up on him. She loved him dearly, and Toni Cameron was no quitter, although she had always felt that living together was wrong. A firm believer in the sanctity of marriage, she had won-

29

dered at times what had possessed her to commit to such an arrangement. But she had no plausible answer except for the fact that she was in love.

Now that it was over, she could see how naïve and gullible she had been, but she had loved the man and had believed every pretty word he said. And he had certainly said enough of them.

"If you'll just be patient and wait until my job is more secure, then we'll get married. We have plenty of time, babe," he had argued. "We have a good thing going for us. Let's not spoil it by getting married."

Or, "Let's get the car paid off before we jump into marriage." Then, "Wouldn't you love to have our furniture paid for first?" On and on the excuses went.

But his excuses soon became old hat to her, and she grew tired of granting him reprieves.

And to add to her misery, her parents were on her case constantly. They made no bones about how disappointed they were in their only daughter, whom they had raised in a home that exemplified love and commitment, and they could not understand her wanting to live with a man without marriage.

So after two long years, Toni couldn't stand the pressure any longer or her own feelings of wanting more from this man. So she had demanded marriage —now or never. Skip had panicked like a cornered animal and chosen never. No doubt this had made her parents ecstatic, but she couldn't say it had done a whole lot for her happiness.

Now she was starting over in a new town with

new surroundings and a totally new outlook on life. She could only hope she wasn't as "tainted" or as "bad a judge of character" as her parents had suggested, and that someday she would find the sort of man she had thought Skip to be when they first met: dependable, trustworthy, and a man of his word.

Maybe, just maybe that was what the problem was. She had just been under too much emotional pressure lately, and she had only imagined that she'd seen that flying saucer last night. She supposed that was possible. The mind could play strange tricks on you at times, and this undoubtedly was one of those times.

She hurriedly made the bed and started for the shower, reminding herself that she wanted to arrive at her new job early today.

It was truly a glorious morning as she stepped out of her side door an hour later dressed in a tailored, light blue linen suit and matching blouse. Her high-heeled navy blue leather pumps made a tapping sound on the concrete drive as she stepped along jauntily. Her mood was much lighter than it had been earlier as she got into her car.

Starting a new job and a new life would be enough to restore anyone's faith in mankind, she reasoned as she tossed a friendly wave to her neighbor, who was just staggering out his back door to retrieve his morning paper.

Her eyes unwillingly paused to study him for a moment. She was a bit taken aback by his appearance this morning. Actually, he looked somewhat like an unmade bed. He was wearing faded pajamas,

31

an old robe with the ties trailing down his sides, and scuffed slippers. His hair looked like he had thrown it up in the air and jumped under it. His eyes were bleary, and he had the sleepy, dazed look of a man who had stayed out too late the night before and now had to pay the piper.

"Good morning," she called out brightly as she put the car in reverse and backed out of the drive. "Beautiful day, isn't it?"

Squinting painfully in the bright sunshine, Zack waved lamely and turned to go back into the house.

She grinned as the car started down the street. Yes, he must have had a big night.

The drive to the courthouse was enjoyable. The town was just the right size for her, and Toni found herself glad that she had picked this area to begin anew. She had chosen the town for no particular reason other than the fact that she had visited a friend here many years ago and had liked the region. It had worked out that the town was also the county seat for Pios County. She found herself wistfully regretting the fact that her friend had moved to California shortly after her visit; at least if Margo still lived here, she would have known someone in town.

Parking proved to be no problem, and shortly after seven thirty Toni was climbing the steep, polished marble stairs of the old courthouse. The building was at least a hundred years old, majestic in design and steeped in Texas history.

Even though the hour was early, the halls were already bustling with activity. The smell of fresh-brewed coffee permeated the air as Toni walked down the corridors looking for the room that housed the Small Claims Court, where she would be working this week.

When she had located the room, she cautiously peeked through the double oak doors and saw a woman dressed in a blue uniform standing behind the judge's bench sorting through some papers. She paused and tapped softly on the door.

Glancing up from her work, the woman smiled. "Yes?"

"Hi, I'm Toni Cameron—the new stenographer?"

"Oh, yes! Toni, come in."

By the time the hands of the old clock behind the judge's bench were approaching nine o'clock, Toni was seated behind her stenographic machine and eager to begin her new job. The fact that she had always possessed exceptional typing skills, along with an unusual love of the judicial system, had made her decide on her profession. Actually, she had dreamed of becoming a judge herself someday, but the idea of law school scared her, so she contented herself with just being in the courtroom with all the action.

The bailiff entered the courtroom and in a deep baritone voice commanded, "All rise."

The small gathering of people did as they were told as he continued. "Court of Pios County is now in session, the honorable Zackery Elsworth Tremayne presiding."

Toni's eyes shot up in surprise as the door to the judge's chambers opened and her new neighbor, looking considerably more presentable and a whole lot more intimidating in his long black robe than when she had seen him earlier in the morning, entered the courtroom.

"You may be seated." Zack picked up a folder of papers lying before him and opened it. "Morgan versus Parks." He paused as he noticed Toni's presence in the room for the first time. A flicker of surprise registered on his face, then he flashed her that cute smile he had before he quickly turned his attention back to his papers.

The morning flew by with amazing rapidity, and Toni was almost disappointed when the noon recess was called. The cases she had heard had been interesting and varied, and she had been completely engrossed in her work.

Somehow, her new neighbor's being a judge still surprised her. Not only was he a judge, he seemed to be a very good one, intent on hearing all the facts of each case no matter how lengthy and how boring they might be.

Walking out into the corridor, she paused and tried to decide which direction the coffee machine would be in. She was not particularly hungry, so she decided to eat the apple she had stuck in her purse that morning and have a cup of coffee during her break.

Locating the women's room, she washed her hands and retouched her makeup, then went in search of the coffee and a comfortable chair.

The vending machines proved to be downstairs, and a long line had already formed in front of them. The smell of sandwiches being heated in microwaves filled the air as she stood and waited her turn.

"I don't know why I put myself through this everyday," the flashy blonde ahead of her muttered as she withdrew a filter-tip cigarette from her purse and lit it. Inhaling deeply, she grumbled again. "The sandwiches taste like they're made out of goat meat when you finally get them."

Toni smiled faintly. "That bad, huh?"

The woman eyed her contemplatively. "You're new around here, aren't you?"

"Yes, this is my first day."

"Then take a tip from me, kid. Stay away from the pastrami. It'll kill you."

A few minutes later, the line seemed to have ceased moving at all, so Toni dropped out and decided to try for coffee again a little later. She found a deserted chair in a quiet corner out in the corridor, where she ate her apple and read the newest issue of *Vogue,* which she had bought earlier.

The crowd around the vending machines had finally cleared out when she rose thirty minutes later and rummaged around in her purse for change.

"Please, allow me."

Toni glanced up to see Zack grinning at her, and her pulse suddenly accelerated for no apparent reason. She certainly hoped she wasn't going to develop a case of adoration for him just because she had always had a thing for judges! she thought irritably. A case of hero worship would be the last thing she needed to complicate her life right now.

"Hi!"

"Hi. Cream or sugar?"

"No, black."

Zack dropped a couple of quarters into the machine and punched a button. A paper cup dropped

35

down and immediately began filling with coffee. "Want to hear how surprised I was at seeing you there in my courtroom this morning?" he prompted.

Toni grinned at him. "I'll bet you weren't half as surprised as I was when I saw you take the bench. Why didn't you tell me you were a judge?"

"Why didn't you tell me you were a stenographer?" he countered.

They both laughed. "I suppose one doesn't run around announcing their profession to their new neighbors, do they?"

"I suppose not." He handed her a cup of coffee and inserted two more coins into the machine. "How was your first night in your new home?"

Her mind immediately conjured up the strange scene in his backyard, but she quickly discarded any idea she might have of telling him about it. "Uh, fine. And how was your appointment?"

"Okay." He smiled and picked up his cup and took a cautious sip. "Things going all right on your first day?"

"So far, so good."

"Well"—he glanced at his watch; Toni noticed it was a very attractive gold Rolex—"I have to run."

"It was nice to see you again," she said sincerely. "See you in court."

He smiled at her again, and she noticed the small dimple on his left cheek again. The unbidden notion that it looked very kissable shot through her mind. She chastised herself immediately for her errant thoughts as he said good-bye, then turned and disappeared back down the corridor as quickly as he had appeared.

Good heavens! She had been so flustered, she hadn't even thanked him for the coffee, she thought irritably.

The afternoon didn't go by nearly as fast as the morning had, but still the day seemed short. She left the courthouse late that afternoon, stopped by a market to purchase a few groceries, then made her way home through the evening rush-hour traffic.

As she stepped out of her car, her eyes unwillingly wandered over to Zack's backyard. She paused and bit her lower lip thoughtfully. Switching the grocery sack to her other arm, she glanced toward his drive cautiously. The Mazda wasn't in the driveway, so he must not be home yet.

Then, before she lost her nerve, she cast one more apprehensive glance around and hurriedly stepped over the hedge and headed around the corner of his house.

This was silly, and she knew it. But if there had been something in his backyard last night, it surely would have left some sort of indication that it had been there; something that big couldn't just come and go and not leave a sign of its visit. If she couldn't find anything unusual, then she would know for sure that it had all been an illusion, and she would dismiss it from her mind once and for all.

Setting her sack down beside the barbecue grill, she bent over and began to carefully examine the area where she thought the object had appeared.

There was nothing irregular there at all. The grass was a lush green, with no evidence of having been exposed to any sort of heat. She had once read an article on flying saucers that said they sometimes

37

radiated great heat; the correspondent told stories of various injuries, ranging from eye damage, burns, radioactivity, partial or temporary paralysis, and various types of physiological disturbances that had occurred in people who had had extraterrestrial sightings.

She shuddered and quickly withdrew her hand from the ground at the thought of radioactivity.

The article had also said that often there was a repulsive odor, like rotten garbage, that lingered for hours after one of their visits. She sniffed the air apprehensively, but there was nothing in the air but the pleasant scent of a lilac bush blooming next to Zack's back porch.

Dropping to her knees, she began to crawl slowly around the perimeter of the yard, pausing to closely inspect the leaves on the bushes for any signs of searing or wind damage. Again, there was nothing to indicate any visitors from outer space.

So preoccupied was she with her mission, she failed to hear the car pull up in the drive.

Minutes later, she had completely circled the yard and was now crawling around the barbecue grill to see if there was anything out of the ordinary there. For some reason, the thing had expressed a great amount of interest in this particular item. Granted, she would have been a little curious about it herself if she hadn't have known what it was.

She lay down flat on her back and stared at the body of the grill. Apparently this had been a home project on Zack's part in his high school days, because it did look rather strange. The round, flat, saucer-shaped kettle had a huge smokestack and sat on four spindly legs that looked almost anorexic. He had not painted it the usual black, but instead had chosen a flamboyant bright red to grace his new creation. No doubt he was proud of it, but it was very funny-looking, even to this earthling's untrained eye.

The sound of someone clearing his throat caused her to quickly snap out of her musings. From her position on the ground, she could see a pair of expensive, immaculately polished men's loafers next to her, and she felt her heart sink as she raised her eyes sheepishly to meet Zack's puzzled stare.

"Oh, hi." She waved at him limply.

He hesitantly waved back. "Hi."

"You're home a little early, aren't you?"

"A little. Are you all right?"

"Sure. Why?"

"You're lying on the ground."

"I know."

"Are you hurt?"

"No, why?"

He knelt down beside her. "No reason. I was just curious about why you were out here lying under my barbecue grill."

Springing to her feet guiltily, she wiped off the seat of her skirt and felt her face flaming with color. "Oh, that. Well." She knew she had to think fast, but her mind wouldn't cooperate. "I was just resting a little before I went home." She grinned weakly. "I hope you don't mind. You have a lovely backyard."

"No. No, I don't mind at all. But wouldn't you rather come up on the porch and rest? I could get us something cold to drink."

"No, no thanks," she refused hastily. "I really have to go in now."

She snatched up the discarded sack of groceries and rushed over to the hedge. "Oh, by the way, thanks a lot for the coffee this morning," she tossed over her shoulder as she lifted up her skirt and straddled the hedge carefully so as not to snag her pantyhose.

Zack watched with anticipation as a slender expanse of leg was bared, then modestly covered back up again.

"My pleasure," he replied.

He stood in his yard with a mystified frown on his face as she scurried up the side porch, unlocked the door, and slammed into her house.

CHAPTER THREE

The following weeks passed swiftly, and life began to settle down to a normal pattern. She loved her job, and she was sure it would only be a matter of time before her loneliness for Skip was a thing of the past.

Somehow, he had found out she was living in Texas, and he had called to see how she was doing. The sound of his familiar voice had brought a fresh round of pain surging through her heart, but when the brief, stilted conversation had ended, she was still relieved that the affair was over.

She had seen very little of her new neighbor in the previous two weeks. She had only been in Judge Tremayne's courtroom twice since she had started work, and since he was practically never home, their paths rarely crossed.

Now that she was finally unpacked and more organized, today would be a good time to repair the damage she had done to his flower bed, she thought matter-of-factly as she stood at the kitchen window Saturday morning and drank coffee. The two deep tire ruts running through Zack's smashed petunia beds were a real eyesore in his otherwise immaculate yard.

He had been very nice and had not said one thing about restoring the flower bed the few times they had talked, but she really felt she should do something about putting it back in order.

A quick trip to the area nursery provided her with the plants she needed to complete the job, and by ten o'clock she was dressed in an old pair of shorts and a halter top busily digging in the warm Texas soil.

Evidently, Zack was still asleep, she mused as her hands energetically tore away the old plants and tossed them aside. And no wonder. The hours he kept would be exhausting to anyone. She had heard of carefree bachelors, but Zack Tremayne was a Superman when it came to his social calendar.

Not that it was any of her business what he did, but living right next door to him, it wasn't hard to keep track of his irregular hours of coming and going.

And the women she had seen going in and out of his house! Whew! They ranged from sophisticated to questionable, in her opinion.

Many nights she had heard the tinkle of ice in glasses and feminine laughter floating out the open living-room window next door as she lay in her bed and tried to get to sleep.

But it was no wonder that he attracted the ladies. He was young, uncommonly nice-looking, sexy, and highly successful.

She even had to admit she was beginning to feel a

certain attraction to him herself, which she found surprising.

In a way, it was an encouraging sign, maybe she was finally getting over Skip. But the last thing she needed was to get involved with a man like Zack, a man who was *obviously* enjoying his freedom.

She had to laugh at her wild imagination, and it suddenly occurred to her that it felt good to laugh again, even if it was at herself.

What in the world had ever made her think Zack Tremayne would be the least bit interested in her in the first place? Although he had been extremely nice to her on their chance meetings, he had never indicated that he wanted to go out with her, let alone get serious about her!

But regardless of how he felt, he had been a good neighbor, and she couldn't complain. She knew he had to be wondering about her after catching her lying under his barbecue grill.

The sound of a screen door banging shut broke into her thoughts. She glanced up and saw Zack stepping off his porch with a cup of coffee in his hand. Fresh from his morning shower, he was dressed in a pair of blue cutoff denims and a white T-shirt that said "Here comes da judge."

"Good morning."

"Hi!"

He surveyed her busy hands. "What's up?"

"Not much. I just thought this would be a good time to work on your flower bed."

Zack yawned and reached up to rub the kinks out of the back of his neck. "That's awfully nice of you, but it isn't necessary. I was going to take care of that myself."

"You shouldn't have to," she dismissed brightly. "I was the one who tore it up."

"Well, I suppose it would go more quickly if we both worked at it." He set his coffee cup down on the ground. "Move over, and I'll give you a hand."

For the next hour they worked alongside each other and chatted first about one thing and then another. She found him to be a very pleasant person, highly intelligent, and with a sense of humor that had her giggling like a schoolgirl from time to time.

". . . and so I asked the defendant why she had spit in the man's face, torn his shirt off, and broken his collector's album of the Beatles over his head, and she told me it was none of my business!" Zack related as he sat back on his heels and rested for a moment.

"And what did you say?" Toni asked, laughing.

"I told her it *was* my business, and then I ordered judgment for plaintiff."

"You didn't!"

"Well, my judgment wasn't based solely on her nasty attitude," he admitted with a chuckle. "The plaintiff had a strong case in his favor."

Toni laughed again, then paused and looked at him, undisguised admiration shining in her eyes now. "You must have a very interesting job." She sighed.

"Yeah, I kind of like it," he admitted.

"Are there any other judges in your family?"

"Yes, my father, and my grandfather, and his father." He grinned. "It's a good thing I like what I do, because I was doomed to follow in their footsteps."

She sighed again and went back to puttering with the new plants. "I thought I wanted to be a judge at one time."

"Oh? Why didn't you?"

"Oh, law school sort of scared me, and I really like being a court stenographer. I think my parents were disappointed that I didn't go on with my education," she confided. "They say I don't have enough get up and go, but that isn't true. I just believe a person has to do what makes them happy, not what someone else wants them to do."

"I agree." He handed her a trowel and wiped his hands on the side of his shorts. "You seem like a pretty smart lady."

"Hah, no, I'm not smart," she confessed, thinking about all the costly mistakes she had made in her life. "But I'm getting more experienced every day."

"Well." Zack stood up and reached for his discarded coffee cup. "It's been good visiting with you again. I'm afraid I have to desert you now. I just have time to mow my lawn, then keep a tennis appointment at one."

She wondered if it was the racy blonde or the flamboyant redhead who would have the pleasure of his company today. "That's okay. I appreciate your help." She stood up and dusted off her hands. "It looks pretty good, doesn't it?"

He surveyed the colorful flower bed with a critical eye. "Yeah, it does. Even better than before," he decided.

He helped her gather up her tools and then walked over to the hedge with her. "Your lawn always looks nice," she complimented. "I don't know where you find the time to keep it in such good shape." And that was the truth, the whole truth, and nothing but the truth; she really didn't know how he did it with his schedule.

"Thanks. I like working in the yard."

They paused at the hedge, and she glanced over his shoulder into his backyard. For a moment, she could still see the strange spaceship hovering . . . glowing. . . .

"That's a nice barbecue grill," she murmured, standing on her tiptoes now to see around his large bulk. Her eyes studied the bright red object intently.

"You think so?" He turned and grinned proudly. "I made that myself in shop when I was a senior in high school."

"No kidding? I don't think I've ever seen one quite like it," she mused. "The legs are so"—she groped for the right word to describe the emaciated gobs of iron—"so creative."

"Yeah." His gaze traveled wistfully over what he obviously considered to be a magnificent work of art. "I was about out of material when I got to the legs, but I think they look all right, don't you?"

"Oh, yes. They're very nice." If—and it was still a big if in her mind—she actually *had* seen something in his backyard that night two weeks ago, then for some reason that thing had been interested in his grill, she was nearly sure of it. But why?

Noting her unusual preoccupation with his grill,

he turned around more fully and followed her gaze with bewilderment. "Something wrong?"

"Wrong?" She quickly blinked to shake her stupor. "Oh, no. I was just looking at your backyard. It's nice."

Nice? He viewed the yard suspiciously. Why was it she kept mentioning his backyard? And now that he thought about it, what was the real reason she had been lying under the barbecue grill that day two weeks ago?

"Yeah, thanks. Yours is nice, too." Actually, both yards were well kept and unusually attractive. Why was she so hung up on his? She seemed like such a nice girl, yet he was beginning to wonder if she was just a little eccentric—or just downright weird.

"Have you ever seen anything strange in it?" she ventured hesitantly.

"Strange?" He looked over his shoulder cautiously. "No. What do you mean, strange?"

"You've never noticed anything . . . big . . . and sort of glowing?" She wasn't about to mention the saucer, but maybe he had seen one himself and would bring up the subject.

His eyes grew a fraction wider. "Big and glowing?" For courtesy's sake, he pretended to think about it for a moment, but felt like an absolute fool for doing so. Of course he hadn't seen anything big and glowing in his backyard! "No, I haven't. Have you?" he asked reluctantly.

"No!" Her denial shot out like a bullet.

He looked at her oddly. "Then why do you ask?"

"Oh, no reason." As quickly as she had brought it up, she suddenly seemed to lose all interest in the

47

subject, and she stepped lithely over the hedge and turned around to smile at him. "Hope you beat the socks off your opponent today."

"Uh—yeah, thanks."

A moment later, she had disappeared around the corner of her house, leaving him wondering what in the world she had been babbling about.

Bananas. That's what she had to be!

Saturday tennis had turned into dinner, and dinner into another late night, Toni thought sourly a couple of days later, and here it was Monday with no letup in sight for His Honor.

She sighed enviously as she proceeded to get ready for bed after another long and exceedingly dull evening. She'd sure like to know what vitamins Zackery took.

Around five, she had heard Zack's car roar up the drive, and he had disappeared into the house for thirty minutes. She had been eating her dinner when she saw him reappear, dressed in a white dinner jacket and black tie. He looked exceptionally handsome. Not that he didn't look that way most of the time. She had no trouble understanding why he seemed to have his choice of female companionship.

The evening had dragged on for her, so by the time the ten o'clock news had come on television, she was ready to call it a night.

For a brief moment she let herself play a harmless little game of what if, as she sat in the window seat and brushed her hair the perfunctory hundred strokes.

What if tonight she were the one out with the

Honorable Judge Zackery Elsworth Tremayne, and they were enjoying a lovely dinner together? He would sit and gaze with adoration into her sultry eyes, while she totally captivated him with her magnetic charm. Then they would dance the night away, their steps lighter than the brush of a butterfly's wing on a delicate rose. He would be attentive, devastatingly virile, and totally absorbed in her loveliness. She would laugh and be so utterly fascinating that by the end of the evening, he would be left wondering how he had ever lived until she had come into his life. And when it came time to part, his sensuous, smoldering gaze would tell her that their time was not over yet—there was more to come, if she wanted it to. . . .

The phone interrupted her meandering thoughts. Still in a dreamy state, she picked up the receiver by her bedside. "Hello."

"Hi! Toni?"

Toni's pulse did a queer little flip-flop at the unexpected sound of his voice. "Yes—Zack?"

"Yeah, hey, I hate to bother you, but I was wondering if you could do me a little favor?"

She sat up a little straighter. "Sure, what is it?"

"You're going to have to speak up a little," he pleaded. The loud background music at the country club made it difficult for him to hear.

"Yes, I'd be glad to do you a favor. What is it?" she repeated loudly.

"I think I forgot to turn my oven off before I left," he confessed. "And it just occurred to me, I'll probably be getting home rather late, and I hate to leave it on all that time. Would you mind running over and turning it off for me?"

Turn off his oven? Her overinflated ego wilted rapidly. Well, turning off his oven was sure a far cry from dancing with him on butterfly wings all night, she thought wistfully, but of course she would be happy to help him. "Sure, Zack. I'll be glad to."

"You're a honey. Thanks a lot." After a hurried explanation of where he kept the extra key, the resounding click of the phone assured her that he was going back to whatever he had been doing with an unburdened mind.

Grumbling under her breath about the unfairness of life, she slipped on her robe and slippers and padded across the living-room floor.

She was sure there had to be a better way to spend an evening than tending to one's neighbor's oven while he was off, gosh knows where, whoop-dee-doing it up!

It was a clear, balmy night as she stepped out onto the side porch and fastened the tie of her robe. The Big Dipper and the Milky Way were strung brightly across the sky as she glanced upward. An occasional light glowed softly in her neighbors' windows, but other than the sound of a dog barking somewhere in the distance, the neighborhood had a sleepy, peaceful air about it.

Stepping down the concrete steps, she headed for the hedge, and in a few moments she was rounding the corner of Zack's house.

Then she came to a sudden, screeching halt.

Her hand shot up to stifle a scream that was

threatening to fill the air as she hurriedly retreated to the safety of the shadow of the house.

It was there again.

Moving so silently that not a leaf on the trees fluttered was a glowing object floating slowly across the housetops, approaching Zack's backyard.

She felt her heart race up to her throat and threaten to cut off her supply of air; she forced herself to take a deep breath and try to gain control of her senses.

Be calm, Toni. This is only another illusion.

Granted, she was more relaxed and rested than when she had thought she had seen it the first time, but maybe her mind was still trying to play tricks on her. That was it. She wasn't seeing a flying saucer at all. She only *thought* she was. Taking another deep breath, she edged over a fraction and cautiously poked one eye around the corner.

Oh, drizzlin's! It was not an illusion! It was there! Only this time, it was a much larger craft than the one she had seen earlier.

At first glance it seemed to be looking for a place to touch down as it crept soundlessly across the treetops and power lines. The lights on the ship were all pointing downward—brilliant yellows and oranges and reds, as if in search of something.

The sheer size of this vessel was overwhelming. It seemed to be well over eighty feet in diameter, and it had a solid, shiny metallic look about it. As she watched, it continued to glide quietly in the darkness like some sort of evil creature that was looking for trouble.

By now it was centered exactly over Zack's back-

51

yard, where it suddenly stopped completely. She watched with bated breath as it hovered motionless for a good five minutes, then slowly began to descend to the ground next to the barbecue grill. Toni wasn't sure if it had actually touched the earth, but immediately following its descent, the lights on the craft flickered and dimmed as if a great amount of power had been used.

Still, the glare from the object was so great she couldn't be sure if it actually had landed or not, and if it had, she knew it would nearly be filling the entire area with its presence.

A few moments later, her suspicions were confirmed as the ship settled gently onto the grass and became ominously still.

By now her legs were threatening to buckle under her as she brought her hand up to cover her mouth. The neighborhood had suddenly grown so quiet, she could have heard a pin drop. Even the dogs had ceased their persistent barking.

She *couldn't* be the only one seeing this strange thing this time! It was too big. Someone had to be witnessing it along with her! She prayed that if it were really there, and not some wild figment of her imagination, that would be the case.

For twenty long, agonizing minutes, the craft sat perfectly motionless. Its lights were now lowered to a dim glow. Not only was Toni afraid to move from her hiding place, but the vessel had her rooted to the spot with fascination. During her periodic cautious peeks around the corner, she had seen no movement in or around the object. To her immense relief, no little green men or frightfully ugly one-eyed creatures came out of the craft to attack her.

Just when she was positive she could stand the suspense no longer, a hatch on the bottom of the ship suddenly opened, and a strange armlike object emerged. The arm had a bright green ball on the end of it, and to her surprise it went immediately to the barbecue grill and began exploring it. Running over every square inch of the grill, it lingered at times, then moved on. She couldn't be sure, but the ball looked as if it had an eye on the bottom of it.

After ten minutes of intense, close scrutiny of the grill, the ball retracted slowly back into the hatch, and it closed.

Another few minutes passed; then the object began to rise. As it came off the ground, Toni could see three massive legs with lights on them; she assumed they were the landing gear that she had been unable to detect earlier. She watched as the vessel reached a height of approximately three hundred and fifty feet; then the legs retracted inside the ship, and it shot upward in a horizontal position and began to pick up speed.

Within seconds, it had disappeared totally from her sight, swallowed up in the starry heavens.

Still unable to move, her gaze continued to span the sky as she followed its path, reluctant for some strange reason to let it go.

Dew had begun to gather on the newly mowed grass, and it was getting cooler now. She felt herself begin to tremble violently as she drew her flimsy housecoat up closer to her neck.

Its speed had been awesome.

As if in a daze, she felt her feet begin to move, taking her in the direction of her house as she continued to cast wondering glances over her shoulder.

Not more than thirty-five minutes had passed since it all began, but it seemed much longer.

How she got there, she couldn't remember, but an hour later she was sitting on her side porch staring up at the sky. The Big Dipper was still there, bright and beautiful, and the Milky Way looked exactly the same as it had earlier. But she felt different somehow: strange and unsettled.

What was out there?

Another planet with a race so advanced in technology that it could silently invade the earth with vessels unbelievable in size and never leave a trace? Or were they, as some people believed, not spaceships from other planets but vessels of terrestrial origin that came from a subterranean race dwelling within the center of the earth itself?

Her gaze remained riveted upward. Who were they, and what in heaven's name did they want with Zack's barbecue grill?

She let out a long, weary sigh. Even more disturbing, what would Zack say when he came home and found his oven still on?

CHAPTER FOUR

By the time Zack's car turned down Fallow Lane, it was close to midnight. Toni was still rooted to her spot on the porch, waiting for him to get home.

She knew he would never believe her when she told him what she had seen, not once, but twice. But she still felt she had to confide in someone, and Zack was the only one she knew well enough to confess such an oddity.

She could only hope he was alone.

Naturally, he wasn't.

The Mazda pulled into the drive, and even before he turned the motor off, Toni could hear the sound of feminine laughter.

The judge must have said something pretty funny because the woman was still giggling as he walked around to the passenger side of the car and opened her door.

Toni sat in the shadows and watched as they proceeded up the drive and disappeared into the house a few moments later.

She was bursting to tell him her news, and yet she knew she shouldn't interrupt his evening. Not only would that be impolite, it would probably annoy him, and she needed him to be in the best possible mood when she told him about the flying saucer.

Biting her lip thoughtfully, she watched the light in his living room come on and heard the sound of music filtering softly out the open window.

Bach, she thought pleasantly. And one of her favorite pieces, too. She closed her eyes and began to absently hum along with the haunting melody under her breath.

Zack walked over to open the window to let in a little more fresh air when his eyes caught sight of Toni on her porch. He leaned forward and tried to make out what she was doing at that hour of the night sitting in the dark in her nightgown.

Humming along with his music. That's what she was doing. Sitting in the dark, humming.

Strange.

He adjusted the window, then turned his attention back to his guest.

Toni snapped out of her dreamy reverie. Rats! What was she doing? She should be thinking of some way to talk to him in private instead of sitting out here in the dark, humming. She rose slowly to her feet. Somehow, she had to get his attention.

Creeping over to the hedge, she carefully stepped over. Glancing about apprehensively, she edged around the corner of the house and paused at his back door. If she could manage to capture his attention without arousing his date's suspicion, then she could tell him about the flying saucer and get it off her mind. Maybe he would have some logical explanation as to why she had seen what she had.

Crouching down, she tiptoed back around the

house and stopped directly under the open window of his living room. Gradually, she peeked up over the ledge to see what they were doing. She felt like such a sneak, and if anyone saw her she would die, not to mention get arrested for being a peeping Tom, but she couldn't take the chance of interrupting him in the middle of some, heaven forbid, romantic interlude. She instantly felt squeamish at that thought, and she was immensely relieved to see that he was standing next to the fireplace talking, while his date was safely seated across the room on the sofa.

Good. Now, if she could only get his attention without the woman noticing.

Jumping up and down, she energetically waved her arms back and forth, praying he would look up and see her. But he was more interested in the topic of discussion than he was in looking out the window and, after a couple of minutes of frantically gesturing with no results, Toni decided she was going to have to try another tactic.

But what? She couldn't just march up to the door in her nightgown and ask if he could come out in the yard for a few minutes. He would think she was crazy.

She couldn't throw a rock through the open window because that would attract the redhead's attention—redhead!

He was with *her* again. Sheesh! What could he possibly see in her? she wondered irritably. This was the second time this week he had taken her out.

Jerking her thoughts back to her immediate problem, she bit her lower lip thoughtfully once more.

If she were really careful, she could stick her hand in the window and wave it around to get his attention. The redhead's back was to her, so that just might work.

Cautiously, she checked to see if the woman was still on the sofa—she was; then before she lost her nerve, she rammed her hand through the open window and wiggled her fingers briskly, then back and forth rapidly.

Zack was about to make a comment when the fingers shot through the window and began their frenzied movement. For a moment he was so stunned by the unexpected intrusion that he fell into a stunned silence.

"And Daddy said what?" the redhead prompted expectantly.

Zack's eyes flew up to the window, and he saw Toni jumping up and down, waving to him.

"Uh—he said—"

The fingers agitatedly motioned for him to retain his composure.

"He said what, darling?" the woman persisted.

"Uh, he said that it wasn't anything to worry about, and he would take care of it," Zack murmured as he managed to regain his voice.

The woman's gaze fastened on the glass she was holding. "That sounds like Daddy. Isn't he precious?"

"Yes, I think a lot of your father." Zack frowned and cocked an inquisitive brow toward the open window.

"You know, Zack, Daddy is very proud of you.

He even predicts you'll be joining him in the Supreme Court someday."

There was only one finger at the window now, and it was beckoning to him pleadingly.

"That's something to think about," Zack conceded quickly. "Uh—would you excuse me for a moment, Karol?"

"Certainly. If you don't mind, I'll just use your bathroom to freshen up a bit."

"No, go right ahead. I'll only be a moment."

Karol disappeared down the hallway as Zack rushed through the kitchen and cracked the door to his back porch open a fraction.

Toni was standing there, an apologetic smile on her face.

"Yes?" He peeked out at her guardedly.

"Hi—I hope I'm not disturbing anything important."

His puzzled gaze surveyed her standing barefooted before him in her gown and housecoat. "Is something wrong?"

"No, except I didn't turn your oven off."

"I noticed that." He looked a little perturbed at her incompetence.

"Aren't you going to ask me why I didn't?" she prompted, hoping he would give her a reason to tell him about the saucer.

He cast a worried glance over his shoulder. "It doesn't matter now. I'm home." He couldn't help but notice how disappointed she looked that he wasn't more inquisitive, so he decided to chance a few more moments with her. "Okay, why didn't you turn the oven off?"

Well, thank goodness he took the bait. "Uh—do you suppose I could have a few minutes with you?" She peered around him warily. "Alone?"

"Can't it wait?" he asked in a hushed voice, glancing worriedly over his shoulder for the second time.

"No," she whispered urgently. "It's very important that I talk to you right now."

"Well, okay," he conceded, slipping out the back door quietly. "But make it snappy. I have company." He couldn't imagine why she would have been jumping up and down in front of his window in her housecoat at midnight, insisting on talking to him; but then, she hadn't been able to give a satisfactory reason as to why she had been lying under his barbecue grill, either.

He was really beginning to wonder about her.

The screen door banged shut behind him as he stepped out onto the darkened porch. "What's up?"

The hair on the back of her neck was what was up, she wanted to say, but instead she cleared her throat nervously. "The reason I didn't turn off your oven was because I was—distracted by something."

"Oh?"

"Yes."

He nodded agreeably. "As I said, that's all right. I've already taken care of it."

"Don't you want to know what I was distracted by?"

No, actually, he didn't. At the moment all he wanted to do was get back to his company before she found him lurking around the porch with a half-dressed woman. "Whatever it was, I'm sure you had a good reason."

"I sure did. It was big—and glowing," she blurted. She held her breath as she watched his face for signs of reaction to her bewildering confession. She glanced around nervously. "And it was in your backyard."

For a moment his polite smile froze on his lips. "What was?"

She edged a step closer to him for fear they might be inadvertently overheard. "You're not going to believe this, but I think I saw a flying saucer in your backyard tonight," she confessed in a frenzied whisper.

"Right." The smile was still there, but his next words were a little stilted. "A flying saucer? In my backyard."

"Yes!" she said breathlessly. "Can you believe it? And you want to hear something really crazy?"

"As if that isn't?"

"No, of course not. I really saw one!" she insisted, then she lowered her voice even more. "I think it's after your barbecue grill!"

His face now registered the reaction of shock that she had expected. "My barbecue grill!"

Hah! Now she really had his full attention!

"You do believe in flying saucers?" she prompted expectantly. "Don't you?"

"No," he stated emphatically.

Her face fell.

Why he should suddenly feel a surge of tender protectiveness toward her he wasn't sure, but strangely, he did.

She stood before him in the moonlight, shivering like a wet puppy in the cool evening air, pale and frightened, trying to convince him she had seen a flying saucer. Not only that, it was supposedly after his barbecue grill to boot.

There was no longer any doubt in his mind. This woman was having some sort of emotional crisis in her life, and as far as he could tell, she had no close family nearby to help her. In fact, he seriously doubted that she had formed any friendships, other than the impersonal one they shared as neighbors, since she had moved here.

"Toni, look." He reached out and took her by her shoulders, aware for the first time of what a delicate, almost fragile frame she had. His hands seemed unusually large on her slender body as she trembled beneath his firm hold. "I don't know what you saw, but trust me, I don't think it was a flying saucer. Hey, are you sure you're all right?" he asked softly as he felt her trembling increase.

"Yes, I'm fine." There was no point in trying to convince him any further of what she had seen. He wasn't going to believe her anyway. "I'm sorry I bothered you," she apologized.

"You didn't bother me." He reached down and tipped her chin up to meet his concerned gaze. "But I'm beginning to worry about you."

"Me?" Her eyes flew up to meet his. "Why?"

He chose his next words carefully so as not to offend her. "I sense you're having a rough time in your life right now. Would you like to talk to me about it? Sometimes, even though another person can't help, it helps to share your misery," he encouraged. "And I'm a pretty good listener. Maybe together we can come up with a solution to whatever it is that's bothering you."

"You think I'm crazy, don't you?" she accused in a voice so low, he could hardly hear her.

And could she blame him? Her story *did* sound pretty farfetched.

"No, not at all. I just want to help you. Will you let me?"

She shook her head wordlessly, deeply touched by his offer. Skip had never wanted to hear her problems, much less offer to help her solve them, and here was Zack, a complete stranger, worried about her welfare.

"Are you sure there isn't something or someone you wouldn't like to talk to me about?" he prompted.

She shook her head once more.

"Well, the offer is always open," he murmured, giving her shoulders an assuring squeeze before he let her go. "Let me walk you home. You're cold."

"No, you have company," she declined softly.

"Karol would understand."

"No, thank you. I'll just run along." She didn't want Karol's sympathy, too!

"It would be no trouble." But his words were barely out of his mouth before Toni had disappeared from the porch and was stepping back over the hedge.

He shook his head worriedly as he watched her slip back to her house and huddle down on the old swing in the shadows of the porch. She was such a strange mixture of woman: all soft and sweet smelling—and very confused.

The sound of the chain creaking back and forth was the only indication that she was there. He stood for a moment, his mind going back over what she had just babbled out to him. A flying saucer? He chuckled softly, then sobered as his gaze sought the perfectly normal, starry heavens.

His brow furrowed thoughtfully. He had never personally believed in flying saucers, but he knew of plenty of people who did.

What had she seen tonight that had made her believe his barbecue grill was under alien surveillance? A plane? A helicopter? Perhaps a satellite or a shooting star? He shook his head musingly and turned back to open the screen door.

Ridiculous. There was nothing strange about his barbecue grill. Unique, maybe, but strange—never.

But the incident had put a damper on his evening, and it wasn't long after that that Toni heard his car back out of his drive. She assumed he was going to take Karol home.

She had no idea why she found such comfort in that thought, but somehow she did.

If she's still in the swing when I get back, I'm going over, Zack promised himself as he deposited Karol at her front door twenty minutes later and said a hurried good night. Toni could deny it all she wanted, but something was upsetting her, and he was going to get to the bottom of the story before he went to bed.

The lights of the Mazda washed over her front

64

porch as he pulled back in the drive around one thirty. The swing was in the corner, well hidden by the old rose trellis, so it was impossible to see if she was still out there, but he sensed she was.

He got out of the car and closed the door softly. "Toni?" he called in a hushed whisper.

"Yes?" Deep within the shadows, the small voice answered quietly.

"Are you still up?"

"Yes." She had been lying down in the swing, thinking. At the sound of his voice, she sat up and straightened her hair.

"You care if I come over for a few minutes?"

"No, come on."

He hopped the hedge, and a few moments later he was sitting down next to her in the swing. "Hi."

"Hi."

"I've been worried about you."

"That's very nice of you, but I'm fine, really."

The chain squeaked as he began to slowly move the swing back and forth. "I thought you'd be in bed by now."

"No, I couldn't sleep."

"It's getting pretty late."

"I know."

"Nice night out."

"Yes, it's beautiful." The roses beside the house were spilling their fragrance into the night air, and she found herself thinking how pleasant it was to sit here beside him and talk. She always felt at ease with him, as if she could just be herself. It had never been that way with Skip. She had forever felt as if she were offending him in some way.

65

"I like the smell of roses, don't you?" he asked.

"Yes, very much."

They swung in silence for a few moments, each lost in the tranquil, sleepy sounds of the night. The neighborhood was dark and peaceful now.

"What did you do before you moved here, Toni?" Zack finally broke the compatible silence.

"Much the same as I do here. I was a court stenographer in Des Moines too."

"You like your work?"

"Very much."

"And your family?"

"I'm an only child with very middle-class, very typical parents. They worry about me a lot," she said thoughtfully. "But I suppose that's natural."

"Yes, I suppose so. My parents are the same way."

"Do you have brothers and sisters?"

"One younger sister, but she doesn't live here anymore. She got married and moved to Los Angeles last summer." Sighing, he locked his hands behind his head and stared up at the ceiling. "Our home was like something out of *Leave It to Beaver.*"

"Oh, that's nice. Mine was too."

"And what about the men in your life?" he asked lightly, turning his attention back to her.

He had decided that that was what was bothering her—it was the only other explanation he could think of, since she liked her job and apparently welcomed the recent move to Texas.

"I would be ashamed to discuss the scarcity of them in view of your active social life," she complained good-naturedly.

He grinned, and she could see the flash of white teeth in the darkness. "A lot of my social life falls under the heading of business," he defended.

"Well, a lot of my social life falls under the heading of Dullsville, U.S.A." she confessed. "I haven't really met anyone but you and Jim since I moved."

"Well, you've met the cream of the crop," he pointed out jokingly.

"Quality, not quantity, huh?"

He grinned again. "Something like that."

They continued swinging for a few moments without saying anything.

"What about before you moved here?" Zack persisted a few minutes later. "Was there a special man in your life before then?"

Toni had never discussed Skip with another person since the relationship had been dissolved. Many of her friends had encouraged her to open up and let her feelings out, but she had chosen to keep her grief to herself. After all, other than providing them with a juicy new tidbit of gossip to toss about, what could they have done? Not even her mother had been able to break her silence. But suddenly, a complete stranger was asking her about her life before Texas, and she found herself wanting to tell him about it.

"I lived with a man by the name of Skip Harden for two years prior to moving here," she said calmly. "I'm not proud of the fact, but I suppose when it comes right down to it, everyone has someone or something in their past that they would like to have the opportunity to do over again. I thought I loved Skip enough to commit myself to that kind

67

of a relationship. I mistakenly reasoned that love was enough. Two years later, I found out it wasn't when I laid down an ultimatum, and he refused to marry me. It was just one of those unfortunate things that happen, and now it's over."

"I'm sorry. That must have been very hard on you emotionally," Zack consoled gently, not at all surprised to hear that's what had been bothering her.

"Yes, it was. But I'll get over it."

"You still love the guy?"

"I'm not really sure. For two years he was my whole life, and that isn't very easy to forget."

"Was there another woman involved in his decision?"

"No, or at least if there was, I never knew anything about it. Skip was just the sort of person who was terrified of legal commitments," she murmured. "In his own way, he loved me. I just wanted more."

"Where is he now?"

"Still in Des Moines. He has his own business there."

The old swing creaked back and forth soothingly.

"What about you?" she asked a few minutes later.

"What about me?"

"Any old live-in love affairs lurking around in your past?"

Zack chuckled. "Are you serious? I may be thirty-seven years old, but my mother would threaten to whip me if she even suspected I was living with anyone of the opposite sex."

Perhaps he wasn't living with anyone, but he certainly was never lacking for female companionship.

She was the one who had to laugh now. "You mean to tell me you're still afraid of your mother?"

"You bet. She can be hell on wheels when she gets on her moral high horse, and I don't want a lecture every time I go over there," Zack admitted without the slightest hesitation.

They both laughed now because Toni knew exactly what he was talking about. Her mother was the same way.

"Well, then, what about being in love? Surely you've been in love before."

"Now you're going to hear something crazy. No, I haven't," he confessed. "Oh, I've been 'in like' with a couple of women, and there was one whom I really respected and looked up to, but I never loved her."

She found that very hard to believe. "You mean with all these women parading through your life, there hasn't been one special one?"

"Hey." He reached over and pinched the tip of her nose playfully. "I grant you that it *may* seem like I'm the town stud, but I can assure you looks can be deceiving. There are a lot of women around my house, but it isn't always what my nosy neighbors think," he said teasingly.

"You mean a lot of it is actually business?" She knew she had no right to ask such a question, but it had slipped out before she knew it.

"Business, personal friendships, and would you believe some of my younger sister's friends still come to me for advice?"

"No, but I have to admit it sounds good." She

had no idea why she was gullible enough to believe that, but she did.

"Actually, I'm very much a gentleman," he murmured coaxingly.

She looked at him. "Gentleman or not, you're still looking for the right girl."

"No, not necessarily," he denied. "I'm very happy with the way my life is right now. If the right one comes along, fine, but if not, then I'll go on just like I am and be happy."

Toni leaned her head back against the swing and closed her eyes. That didn't surprise her. He was like all men—commitment was a dirty word they shied away from. "Well"—she yawned and sat up a few moments later, fatigue beginning to overtake her now—"I suppose I should be going inside. We both have to go to work tomorrow."

"Yeah, I have to be there early, but I wanted to make sure you were all right before I went in."

"That was very nice of you, but I'm fine, really."

He reached over and tipped her face up to meet his. "Are you sure?"

"Positive. I should have never mentioned the flying saucer to you in the first place."

"No, I'm glad you did, but I think after you get a good night's rest, you'll look back on the incident and realize what you saw was only a plane or something of that sort," he said comfortingly. "From what you tell me, you've been under a great deal of stress lately, and sometimes that makes our minds play funny little tricks on us."

"Yes, I know." Even in the dark, his eyes were beautiful, she thought absently. Sexy, bedroom eyes.

"Then you agree?"

"That I didn't see a flying saucer?"

"Yes."

She sighed and pulled her head away from his hand. "No, I'm almost positive that's what it was, but if you don't want to believe it, I understand."

"Toni!" Just when he had begun to think he was reaching her. "Come on. You didn't see a flying saucer! You saw a plane."

"No, it wasn't a plane. I think it was a flying saucer," she insisted. "But I could be wrong."

"Good—at least you admit you could be wrong."

"But I have to tell you, it wasn't the first time I saw it. Whatever it was, there was another one almost like it in your backyard two week ago." She might as well tell it all and get it over with. "That's when it first noticed your barbecue grill."

"Good Lord." He groaned and buried his hands in his hair. They were back to the barbecue grill again! *"If* there was something unusual in my backyard—and I'm not about to admit that I think there really was, except for the sake of argument—why in the world would it want my barbecue grill?"

"I don't know. Maybe because it's so funny looking," she hazarded a careful guess.

He bristled like an old porcupine at the suggestion. "Funny looking! What's funny looking about it?"

"Nothing, really. It's just not your normal, run-of-the-mill grill." She hedged for fear of hurting his feelings.

"I should say not." He sat up straighter and fidgeted with the cuffs on his shirt irritably. "It may not be a Weber, but I think it's pretty darn nice."

"I do, too," she agreed eagerly. "It's really nice; I didn't mean that. I only meant, you don't see one like it in every yard."

"I know. That's what I like about it." He ran his fingers through his hair once more. He couldn't believe he was sitting here actually defending his barbecue grill against an invasion from outer space.

"I know this is all hard to believe. I thought I had dreamed it myself, but when it came back tonight, I was almost certain it was real," she tried to justify her claim and apologize all at the same time.

He shook his head wordlessly. What could he say to a woman who had *obviously* popped her cork?

Deciding that he, too, had had more than he could take in one night, she stood up and prompted him to his feet. She knew how unnerving all this could be, and she couldn't blame him for being confused. "I know this is all very hard to absorb, but after you get a good night's sleep, you'll feel better," she said soothingly as she took his hand and led him to the hedge.

"But—"

"No buts. Just forget I said anything about it. I'm sure whatever it was has satisfied its curiosity, and it probably won't ever return. Although, come to think of it, it wasn't the same flying saucer that was here last time. This one was much bigger."

He looked at her vacantly. "Bigger?"

"Yes." She nodded solemnly. "Nearly twice the size."

"Oh, Lord."

"But don't worry about it," she said again. "I'm sure we'll probably never see it again."

"But—" Forget there was a flying saucer trying to steal his barbecue grill? She must be kidding. He cast a pitiful glance at his grill sitting tranquilly in his backyard. "But—"

"And, Zack, thanks for being such a good neighbor. I really appreciate it." She stood on tiptoe and kissed him lightly on the mouth. Gosh, he tasted even better than he looked.

She wasn't sure how it happened, but suddenly the kiss that had started out as an affectionate peck swiftly changed course on her.

Their mouths touched briefly, then all of a sudden they were kissing—really kissing. Her head grew light as her arms wound around his neck, and with a low groan he pulled her up closer to him.

The kiss continued to deepen until her knees grew weak. It was several long, incredibly spine-tingling moments before either one of them could summon up the courage to break the torrid embrace.

"Uh . . ." Zack's voice was shaky when they finally parted a few moments later. "I think you'd better go in before I make myself out to be a liar." The kiss had left him shaken and wondering what had hit him.

"About being a gentleman?"

"That's right—about being a gentleman." He leaned down and touched his lips to hers again gently. "Good night, my funny little neighbor."

"Good night, Zackery." She backed toward her house, reluctant to leave his company.

"Uh, Toni?"

73

"Yes?"

"Do you really think you saw a flying saucer?" he prompted. "I mean—are you positive?"

She nodded her head slowly up and down. She hated to upset him further, but after all, he had asked, and she wasn't about to lie to him. "Yes, I'm sure that's what it was, all right."

He was still standing at the hedge, stunned, as she slipped inside her house.

A flying saucer! His eyes searched the darkness helplessly. She had seen a flying saucer?

And it was after *his* grill?

CHAPTER FIVE

Yes, the more she thought about it, the more sure she was that what she had seen last night in Zack's backyard had indeed been a flying saucer.

But like thousands of others, she was going to have a hard time trying to convince anyone else of it.

She sat in the public library the following evening eagerly thumbing through articles on actual public sightings of unidentified flying objects. Book after book had been written on the puzzling subject, and she sat spellbound as she read them, one by one.

There were those who contended that the unexplained phenomena had been seen even as early as biblical days. Another report suggested it all actually began around 1947, when a businessman from Boise, Idaho, was flying his private plane, he encountered nine disk-shaped objects estimated to be traveling seventeen hundred miles per hour speeding by his window. The objects reportedly weaved in and out of the mountain peaks with great mobility and then disappeared.

According to the records, there reportedly have been significant UFO sightings over every major

American and European city and every major military installation around the world, including the American Strategic Command and various nuclear installations since that fateful day in June 1947. Consequently, the Air Technical Intelligence Center of the Air Force set up Project Bluebook, a program designed for high-priority, high-security investigation of reported flying saucers. Since then, literally thousands of people have reportedly witnessed the strange occurrences in the sky.

Something was up there, but exactly what?

Toni closed the last book slowly and sighed. Whatever these UFO's were, she had seen one of them, and even though he was going to think she was crazy, she had to go back over to Zack's this evening and talk to him. It wasn't the ideal solution to this sticky problem, but since she knew no one else in town who would listen to her, she would just have to take the chance that he would lend her his ear once more.

She thought about reporting the sightings to the proper authorities but quickly discarded that. She wasn't quite ready to face what would undoubtedly be a condescending attitude toward her. Zack might not believe her, but so far he had been kind about it.

She drummed her fingers thoughtfully on the table. Then again, he would probably strangle her if she showed up on his doorstep again. She had interrupted him and what's-her-name last night, and although he had been polite about her intrusion, he might not be as considerate if she did it again.

Actually, there was even a minuscule chance he wouldn't be doing anything this evening.

Minuscule, but not totally impossible.

Oh, well, she had to take the chance.

Scooping up the armful of books, she took them to the counter and applied for a library card.

Ten minutes later, she had the card plus the ammunition she needed to convince Zack she wasn't completely off her rocker. She dumped the books into the back seat of her car and started home.

It was a little after nine when she pulled into her drive and glanced hopefully in the direction of his house. Wonders of wonders, the Mazda was sitting in the drive. Of course, that didn't necessarily mean that he was home or alone, but it looked favorable.

She got out of the car and gathered up the books, still keeping a watchful eye on the residence next door. There was a soft light burning in the living room, but the window was closed. Since the weather had turned hot and sultry, he had probably turned the air conditioner on, she reasoned. Still, she wished the window were open so she could hear if he had company.

But surely he didn't. Even Superman had to rest occasionally.

A moment later, she found herself on his back porch trying to balance the cumbersome load of books and find a free hand with which to knock on the door.

The best way to handle this was with sheer finesse, she decided as she briskly rapped on the frame of the screen. When he opened the door, she wouldn't wait to be invited in. She couldn't take the chance that he would try to find an excuse to dis-

77

miss her and send her on her way before she had talked this baffling situation out with him.

No, she would simply breeze by him as if she were expected, and hope for the best.

She knocked again.

Maybe he wasn't home after all. Maybe ol' redhead what's-her-face had come by and picked him up this evening, and they had gone out together again. That idea annoyed her and she hammered louder. What he could possibly see in that woman was beyond her.

The sound of footsteps coming across the kitchen floor a few moments later laid to rest her fear that he wasn't home. Seconds later, the back door was cautiously opened a fraction.

"Yes?"

"Hi."

Recognizing his neighbor as the untimely intruder, Zack worriedly eyed the stack of books she was carrying as he opened the door a little farther. "Hi."

"Boy, I'm glad to see that you're home," Toni said with a sigh of relief as she hurriedly pushed her way by him and entered the kitchen. "For a minute there, I thought you had gone out again."

"No, I'm home, but—"

"Now, don't worry," she assured him as he shut the door and began to trail helplessly behind her. "I won't stay but a minute, but I stopped by the library on the way home from work this afternoon and picked up some books on the subject of—" She paused, debating whether to call them flying saucers in his presence. Last night he had made it clear he didn't believe in their existence. "You know what," she improvised quickly, "and I knew you would be interested in what I've learned."

"Toni, I—"

"Honest, I'll only take a few minutes of your time, Zack," she pleaded. "I just need someone to talk to. This whole thing has me unnerved—" Her voice broke off as she burst into the living room. "Oh, dear, I'm sorry. I didn't think you had company tonight."

The redhead was seated at a small table set for two, complete with fresh flowers and candles burning low in elegant crystal holders, sipping a glass of white wine.

Toni felt her heart sink and her face flood with color. Obviously, they were just about to have dinner, and she had interrupted them again.

Zack's guest glanced up in surprise at their hasty entrance and set her glass quickly down on the table. There was an appalling silence for a few moments as the three of them each waited for the other to speak. It was Zack who found his voice first.

"Uh, Karol, this is my next-door neighbor, Toni Cameron. Toni, Karol Massenburg."

Toni shifted the books around to one arm and smiled guiltily as she stepped over to take Karol's hand. "Hello, Karol. I'm sorry to disturb you. I didn't realize Zack had company."

Karol smiled politely. "It's quite all right."

"Well, I'll just be running along." Toni backed toward the safety of the doorway, still trying to juggle the mound of books she was holding.

Zack stepped forward just as they were all about

to tumble to the floor and quickly helped her redistribute her load.

"Thanks." She smiled up at him gratefully.

"Was there something important you needed to talk to me about?" he asked.

It was clear to Toni that he was only being polite, and she wouldn't dream of interfering with his evening. "No, nothing that can't wait."

As she backed toward the doorway once again, one of the books toppled off the stack and slid across the room in front of Karol's stylish alligator pumps.

Karol reached over and picked up the book and read the title with interest. *"Flying Saucers?"* She looked at Toni. "Are you interested in UFOs?"

Before she could assure her she most certainly was, Zack hurriedly intervened. "Uh, Toni's an amazing lady. She has a little bit of interest in all subjects." He shot Toni a warning look that said, *Don't start in on the flying saucers again!* "Let me help you to the door with those books."

It was plain he didn't want her discussing with Karol what she thought she had seen in his backyard. "Well, I find the subject interesting," Toni admitted, sending a resentful glare back in his direction.

"You know, it's strange, but I do, too," Karol confessed. "Once when I was in college, I did a paper on flying saucers. It was interesting and thought-provoking. Tell me, do you believe they actually exist, or do you think that they are experimental aircraft belonging to our government?"

"You know, I've thought a lot about that lately."

Toni maneuvered around a scowling Zack and sat down in the chair across from Karol. She peered at Karol anxiously. Maybe she had misjudged this woman completely; she might have a brain under all those flaming tresses after all! "But I really don't know. What do you think?"

"Now, Toni," Zack protested lamely, "Karol and I were about to have dinner—"

"I honestly don't know, either," Karol admitted, totally ignoring Zack's grumbling. "Zack, dear, where are your manners? Maybe Toni would like to join us in a glass of wine?"

"No, she wouldn't," Zack said quickly. "She has to be running along."

Toni looked at him sharply. "No, I don't. I mean, I could join you—if Karol doesn't mind." She *had* misjudged her. Here was a highly intelligent woman wanting to discuss something that was very close to Toni's heart at the moment.

"I don't mind at all," Karol assured her as she picked up the remaining books and began to thumb through them. "I find the subject of flying saucers simply fascinating, don't you, Zackery?"

"No, I don't believe in them myself," he grumbled as he poured a tulip-shaped goblet of Chablis and handed it to Toni.

She smiled at him sweetly and accepted the glass. She knew he wasn't overjoyed about her staying, but if Karol wanted to discuss UFO's with her, then she wanted to hear what she had to say.

"You know, I read an interesting theory about the big blackout along the whole eastern seaboard in the sixties," Karol mused. "You remember when the lights went out in New York City?"

Toni nodded. "Sure."

"They were never able to come up with a satisfactory reason as to why that blackout occurred, but there was supposedly a formation of flying saucers sighted over the city that night."

"No kidding?" Toni's eyes widened. "That was a horrible blackout. People were stuck in elevators and subways for hours."

"Yes, it was a frightening situation for many."

"It wasn't all that bad. A lot of babies were born nine months later," Zack quipped, slowly coming around to the fact that Toni was going to stay for a while.

"Zackery!" Karol gave him a reprimanding look, then went on with her observations. "Flying saucers are supposed to produce electromagnetic interferences of various kinds. They've reportedly been known to interrupt ignition systems, automobile lights, and radios, and to even turn off car engines. When the saucer has passed over, or shut off whatever directional power they have applied, the engines have restarted by themselves."

"But could they cause such a massive power outage as the one that occurred in New York?" Toni asked incredulously.

"Certainly not," Zack scoffed. "Ladies, I'm not saying there isn't something up there, but it has to be something our government doesn't want known, and if that's the case, then it has to be for defense purposes, and people ought to let the defense department do their job."

"But, Zack," Toni protested, "the sightings are being recorded in all climates and countries."

"The government gets around in strange places, Toni."

Karol shrugged. "Of course, it's only a theory concerning that particular blackout along the eastern seaboard, but who knows? In my research, I've read fascinating stories of people who say they have actually been abducted by the alien visitors and used for experimental purposes before they were released. And what about all those people every year who simply disappear off the face of the earth and are never heard from or seen again? What happens to those people?"

Toni shuddered at the thought. She had read those same stories. There were even people who had radiation burns and other horrifying side affects to substantiate their claims of having had close encounters. But still the public was skeptical.

"Some people disappear and are never heard from or seen again because that's the way they want it," Zack contended, "not because some flying saucer has come down and carried them away."

"Then you think that people who say they have seen a UFO are crazy?" Toni asked worriedly.

Zack's eyes softened. "No, I didn't mean that. I only meant that what they saw must have a reasonable explanation."

"Such as?"

"Optical illusions, weather balloons, experimental aircraft, conventional aircraft, atmospheric conditions, emotional stress—I could go on and on."

Emotional stress. There it was again. He thought

she was under some sort of emotional stress and was seeing things.

"Hey, look. We could sit here and debate the question all night and never come up with an answer that would suit all of us," he pleaded. "It's nearly ten o'clock, and we still haven't eaten yet. I'm hungry."

The night was not exactly going as planned, and he was tired of hearing two women chatter about the pros and cons of flying saucers.

Toni immediately jumped up from her place at the table, painfully aware that she had overstayed her welcome. "Oh, of course. How inconsiderate of me."

"Now, wait," Karol protested. "Don't go yet." She glanced at Zack expectantly. "Why, I'll bet Toni hasn't eaten yet, either, have you?"

"No, but I wouldn't dream of interfering with your evening." Toni shot a smile at her neighbor, knowing full well that Karol was going to insist she stay. "I'll just be running along."

"You wouldn't be interfering," Karol denied. "Would she, Zackery darling?"

Zack shrugged, resigned to the fact that no matter what he thought, he was probably going to be overruled anyway. "No, not at all. We would be happy to have you join us, Toni."

Well, as long as it was put that way, she saw no reason to decline the offer. And besides, she *was* getting hungry.

"That's very nice of you," she accepted gratefully. "But I insist on helping."

"There's no need—"

"No, really. I insist." She grinned at him. "What's on the menu?"

"Steaks."

"Is the grill ready?"

"Yes, *if* some little green men haven't come down and stolen it," he remarked dryly.

"Then I insist you let me cook them." She ignored the not-so-funny joke. She was aware that she had a perfectly sympathetic ear in Karol Massenburg, but for some reason she wasn't quite ready to let anyone other than Zack know about her own personal experience—at least, not yet.

"There is no need for that. I am perfectly capable of cooking our steaks."

But Toni wouldn't hear of it. "No, you've been so nice about me spoiling your evening, I insist on fixing our dinner. You and Karol just sit in here and enjoy yourselves while I grill the steaks." She turned to Karol. "How do you like yours cooked?"

"Rare."

"And yours?" She looked at Zack.

He shrugged. "Done."

"One rare and one done, coming right up!"

Toni scurried out to the kitchen, her mind still lingering on flying saucers. It was a stroke of luck to find someone as knowledgeable about the subject as Karol was, and she hoped during dinner that they could pursue the subject further. By then she might even be ready to confide in Karol about her own strange encounter.

An hour later, Toni and Karol were still chattering over their steaks while Zack sat quietly and ate his dinner. Toni noticed that he had barely said a word during the meal, and she became concerned.

"Is your steak all right?" she inquired pleasantly.

"It's fine," he said curtly.

She absently went back to the discussion of a well-publicized case several years ago concerning a couple who had reportedly had their car blocked on a road by a strange craft in September 1961, at which point they claimed to have lost control over their own volition. She opened one of the books she had brought over and began to read aloud. "The couple contended that five occupants of the craft had taken them into the alleged spacecraft, where they were given a complete medical examination and then released. They were able to clearly recall all but the two or so hours they had spent in the craft itself. That part of their story was incomplete, and it was not until two years later, when they both agreed to undergo hypnosis, that they learned what had occurred during that time."

"I remember the case well," Karol said enthusiastically. "They didn't tell anyone but close friends and relatives what had happened to them, but when the man began to experience health problems after the alleged incident, he decided to see if there was any emotional basis for the ulcer he was experiencing. He was referred to a psychiatrist, and only then did the true story about their encounter begin to unfold."

"How terrible for those people," Toni murmured. "It says here that the craft was disk-shaped with red lights and a double row of windows—and oh my gosh. Inside the windows they could see the silhouette of human-type figures . . . and later on they describe the occupants as being short, and all dressed alike with very large eyes and almost no nose and grayish skin."

Zack cleared his throat impatiently and pushed away from the table; half of his meal remained on the plate. "If you ladies will excuse me."

Karol glanced up at him. "Where are you going?"

"If you two insist on carrying on this discussion, I have some briefs to work on," he replied curtly.

Now Toni did feel bad. Not only had she barged in on him and completely ruined his evening with Karol, but she had dominated the entire meal with tales of flying saucers, which he clearly did not believe in.

She closed the book she had been reading from and immediately rose. She smiled her apology at Karol. "That won't be necessary, Zackery." She decided that from now on she would use his full name when addressing him, the same way Karol did. It sounded so much classier. "I really must be going now."

"Must you?" Zack nearly jumped across the table to assist in her departure.

She shot him a dirty look. "Sorry, but I really must."

"I wish you wouldn't. If Zackery's going to work on his stuffy old papers, you might as well stay. We can have coffee in the living room," Karol invited.

Well, there was one thing she was sure of. Zackery would not be working on his stuffy old papers if she cleared out of here. "No, I really must be going." She began to hurriedly gather up the books that were now scattered about the table.

"Do you need some help with those?" Zack offered, still obviously eager to see her go.

"No, thank you. I'll make it just fine." She said a hurried good night to Karol and started for the back door. Zack followed and courteously held the door open for her.

"You sure you don't need any help?"

"No. But Zack—" She paused and turned to look up at him. He was at least five inches taller than she was and definitely a very handsome man. For a moment she felt an unexplained wave of affection for him. Maybe it was because he was the only one she knew in town, or maybe it was just because he had been so nice to her. Whatever it was, she felt greatly indebted to him at that moment. "I'm really sorry about spoiling your evening. You should have just told me to go home."

"I wouldn't do that, and you didn't spoil my evening," he insisted, but she couldn't help but notice the look of genuine concern he was giving her. "I just hope you don't let this flying saucer thing get you down."

"I won't, and I'm sorry again if I bothered you."

He chuckled softly and reached out to tweak her nose, a habit that was beginning to become a ritual with him. "You're no bother. How many times do I have to tell you that?"

She grinned back at him and sighed. "Thanks. I don't want to be." For just a tiny moment, she forgot that Karol was in there waiting for him, but then she remembered her manners. "Karol's very nice."

"Yeah, she is. Maybe we can all do it again sometime." She knew he was teasing her now, but she didn't care. "Only next time, leave the flying saucer books at home and bring along a date."

"Okay. Will do." She winked at him playfully.

"Try and get a good night's sleep."

"I will." She turned and started down the steps, then turned once more to face him. "Oh, Zackery?"

"Yeah?"

"Now, don't get mad," she warned, "but to be on the safe side, I really think you should put your barbecue grill in the garage."

"Thanks, I'll think about it."

"Good night."

"Good night."

CHAPTER SIX

Well, why not take him up on his offer, even though she knew full well he had only been teasing her when he had suggested they get together again?

He hadn't exactly meant that *they* get together, but what the heck. Somehow she just knew that if she waited for Zackery Tremayne to ask her out, she might have a long wait.

Toni was still flirting with the idea of seizing the initiative and asking him out herself as she dawdled over coffee in the cafeteria the following morning; she saw him come in with two other men and take a seat across the room from her. It would be highly uncharacteristic of her to do such a brazen thing, but lately she hadn't been herself at all.

Her mother's favorite proverb suddenly popped to mind. "Nothing ventured, nothing gained."

If that were true, what would she have to lose?

It was all she could do to keep her eyes on the morning news and off the handsome picture he presented as he fell into a deep conversation with his colleagues. He was dressed in a pair of dark trousers, a pale green shirt, and a charcoal-gray sweater vest. The color of his shirt made his eyes look like two sparkling gems beneath his heavy brows as he talked and gestured with his hands about some point he was trying to make.

To be honest, it was all she could do to keep from outright staring at him.

For just a brief moment she tried to imagine what his eyes would be like if they were gazing into hers over candlelight and soft music—or passionately after just having made love to her. She felt a tiny knot in her stomach tighten. She could well imagine that a woman would be powerless if he decided to turn on his charm. She took another sip from her cup as her eyes peeked discreetly over the rim.

Yes, green was definitely his color.

"Ya through with that sugar, lady?" A burly arm reached in front of her and latched on to the container sitting before her.

"Yes, sure." She moved back as the arm zipped back under her nose and disappeared.

But then again, he looked great in blue, too. She absently went back to her daydreaming. Day before yesterday, he had worn a three-piece blue suit that had looked like a million dollars on him. And last week, he had worn a shade of brown that looked good enough to eat.

Would he think she was overstepping her bounds if she did suggest that they go out for dinner some night?

She sighed and let her gaze drop away reluctantly.

Probably. Zack didn't seem the type who would appreciate a woman asking him out. Oh, he would be polite, but he would make all kinds of excuses as to why he couldn't go. She knew the type well.

Now Skip, on the other hand, would not only have been elated at such an occurrence, but he would be bragging all over town about the fact that a woman had tried to put the make on him.

She laughed mirthlessly under her breath and reached for her purse to leave. But then, Skip was about as different in nature from Zackery as black was from white.

Zack left his table at about the same time Toni decided to step out into the aisle, and they collided with each other rather soundly.

"Oh, I'm sorry," she apologized.

"Oh, pardon me, Toni. Hey, how're you doing?" Zack steadied her with two large hands and grinned down at her. "You're about to get run over, lady."

"Yeah." She grinned back at him. "I didn't see your headlights."

They fell in step with each other as they walked toward the register, still chatting away.

"How are you this morning?"

"Fine, thank you."

"Didn't see any flying saucers out your window last night?"

"None at all," she returned good-naturedly, realizing he was only teasing her again. "Your grill still in your backyard?"

"It was the last time I looked."

"Lucky you."

"I'd say," he bantered back, winking. "I'm pretty attached to my barbecue grill, and I'd sure hate to lose it."

"I can't blame you. It is one of a kind."

Then, before she could object, he reached over and took her check out of her hand and laid it down with his. She immediately rummaged around in her billfold and extracted a dollar to give to him, but he only brushed her hand away and kept on talking. "My pleasure. Nice day out, isn't it?"

"I thought it was raining."

"It is, but I love rainy days," he confessed.

When the bill was taken care of, he held the door open for her, and they exited out into the corridor of the courthouse.

"Do you have court this morning?" she asked conversationally as she sought to keep up with his long strides down the polished hallway.

"Not until this afternoon. How about you?"

"Yeah, nine o'clock." She glanced at her watch and quickened her pace in the direction of the three elevators in the main lobby.

"You coming?" She stepped in the elevator and turned to face him expectantly.

"No, I have business out of the courthouse this morning." He smiled at her unexpectedly as he stepped halfway into the car and reached out with one hand to prevent the door from closing.

Suddenly she felt almost bashful as he continued to appraise her more closely. His eyes were running over her in a most peculiar way, almost as if he were really noticing her for the first time. "I like that dress," he complimented. "You look good in red."

And she did. Darn good, he thought silently. Funny, but she was one of the prettiest ladies he knew. She always looked the same when he saw her,

93

neat and fresh, and her clothes always fit her just the right way—not too tight, not too loose—just right.

"Thank you. I was just thinking how nice you look in that particular shade of green, myself," she returned shyly.

"Thank you." His smile was so sexy, it nearly took her breath away.

Well, at least his noticing her dress was encouraging. Maybe he had come to think of her as more than a neighbor and would ask her out now. But a few moments later he dashed that small hope. Apparently the dress was the only thing that had caught his attention, because he merely winked at her again and let his hand fall away from the door. "Well, you'd better get up there. It's almost nine."

Like a streak of lightning, her hand shot out to prevent the door from closing as she hurriedly gathered up all the confidence she could muster. By golly, she was going to take the bull by the horns and ask him out. He might refuse, but that was the worst he could do. He couldn't burn her at the stake. All he could do was say no, and she was fully prepared for that, so she might as well take the plunge and ask him on the slim hope that he didn't already have other plans made for the evening.

"Say, Zack?"

His eyes traveled discreetly but with definite male appreciation over the way her dress was now stretched tightly over her breasts as she endeavored to keep the door from closing in his face. "Yes?"

She swallowed uneasily and plunged on before

she lost her nerve completely. "How would you like to have dinner with me tonight?"

"I'd like to," he accepted without a moment's hesitation. He had been wanting a chance to talk to her in private. This flying saucer business was beginning to worry him, and he wanted to encourage her to get to the root of whatever was bothering her and causing her to see things that weren't there.

"Well, that's all right," she hurriedly rushed on, "I knew you would probably already have plans made and—" She paused in midsentence, his words belatedly sinking in. "You'd like to?" She was almost gaping at him now. He had actually said yes!

"Yes, but—"

Oh. For a minute, she had actually thought he was going to accept! "But?" She wasn't a fool. He was going to be polite and say he'd love too but—

"I was just going to say I'll probably be in court until around seven, but I'm free after that if you are."

She was so floored by his easy acceptance of her proposal, she could barely believe her luck. "Uh— well, sure, seven would be fine with me."

"Good. You want me to come by for you?"

"No, I thought we might go out for Chinese food —that is, if you like Chinese food."

Since she had never asked a man out for a date before, she was rather unsure of the procedure, but he seemed to think she was doing okay. At least he hadn't turned around and run yet.

"I'll eat anything that won't eat me first," he admitted with a boyish grin. "Chinese food sounds great."

"Then I'll pick you up outside a little after seven," she rushed on before he could change his mind.

Then her conscience started nagging her. It really wasn't very nice of her to exclude Karol, especially since she wasn't exactly sure what the relationship between the two of them actually was.

No, if she was going to do this, she would do it fairly and include the redhead in the invitation.

But she wouldn't be held accountable if Zack happened to be more attracted to her than Karol.

"Do you think we should ask Karol, too?"

"Karol?" He looked at her blankly. "No, I don't think so. I think we're old enough to be on our own, don't you?"

"Yes!" And she knew instantly she had said that too quickly. "I mean, yes, I just thought she might enjoy coming along," she said more serenely.

"She'd appreciate the thought, but I think she has other plans tonight, anyway." He grinned at her knowingly.

Naturally, or why else would he have agreed to come to dinner with her?

"Well, whatever you think." Who was she to argue? If he didn't want Karol along, he didn't want her along.

With a brief wave of his hand, he stepped aside to let a newly arrived couple enter the elevator, and seconds later the door closed and the car began its ascent to the third floor.

Slumping against the elevator wall, Toni let the tension slowly drain out of her, delighted that she had found the nerve to ask him out. And for the first time in a very long time, she had the urge to laugh out loud for no reason at all.

Ever since childhood, she had always had an annoying habit of giggling when she was nervous about something. She supposed that's why she was feeling that way now; she *had* been extremely nervous about asking Zack out. She had fought hard all her adult life to control that strange habit, inwardly cringing whenever she thought about how people had reacted to her odd behavior. They would always look at her as if she were crazy when she would dissolve in a fit of giggles during a crisis, and who could blame them? After all, if a person is upset about something, isn't it the normal procedure to wring their hands or cry or stomp their foot in exasperation? But not for Toni. She would stand and giggle!

The man standing in front of her had his hat on at a jaunty, almost cocky, angle and for some reason that struck her as unusually funny. She was fighting back a chuckle when the smell of the lady's perfume standing with him settled over the small car and nearly sent her into fits. It was heavy perfume, stifling actually, and somehow, even though the pair wasn't the least bit unusual, they made a funny-looking sight to her.

Before she could stop herself, a horrifyingly loud laugh escaped her lips.

The man turned sideways and looked at her oddly. She steadfastly ignored his stare and turned her eyes upward, praying she could keep a firm grip on her wavering composure.

But a few seconds later, she guffawed again before she could get herself under control.

As the couple left the elevator, they were still looking at her as if she needed a padded cell, and she was still giggling.

Brother! she thought miserably, her whole body still vibrating with ill-concealed merriment.

If the mere thought of one casual date with Zack Tremayne was going to affect her like this, she would hate to think of what an entire evening alone with him would do to her!

"Are you about ready to strangle me?" Zack hurriedly ducked into the car to avoid the rain a little after seven thirty that evening. "I'm really sorry. I got tied up and couldn't get away."

The drops peppered down onto the windshield as Toni pulled away from the curb and eased her car into the ongoing traffic.

"I figured that's what happened, but don't worry about it. I had a book to read while I waited."

"It's really coming down." Zack looked uneasy as he unbuttoned his raincoat and glanced over at her. "I'd be happy to drive if you want me to."

Toni grinned. "Do woman drivers make you nervous?"

"No, you're doing a great job," he assured. "I'm just used to driving on dates."

They made small talk as they drove to the restaurant, which was about ten minutes away from the courthouse. Toni had called earlier and made reservations, so when they arrived they were shown directly to their table and seated.

"Hey, this is great," Zack said. "I've never been out with a woman before."

"Oh? What have you dated? Ducks?"

"No, you know what I mean. I've never been taken out. I think I'm going to like it."

"Good. I think I'm going to like taking you out," she said, then hurriedly picked up her menu and buried her flaming face in it.

"What sounds good?" Zack had to chuckle at her candor as he picked up his menu. They mulled it over together. "Chow Mein, Egg Foo Yong, Green Pepper Steak, Chicken Livers with Fried Rice . . ."

She wrinkled her nose in distaste, and he laughed. "You hate liver, too?"

"That's putting it mildly." Resuming her study of the menu, she found herself squinting as she tried to make out the small print in the dim light of the restaurant. "I guess I'm going to have to give up and start wearing my glasses again," she complained.

"The old eyesight going on you?"

"It seems that way. I've been thinking about contact lenses."

After much discussion, they finally settled on Cashew Chicken and Fried Rice with a pot of hot tea.

"We're not very adventurous," Zack said teasingly. "I think I would have loved the Barbecued Mandarin Duck with Cherry Sauce."

It was amazing to her just how comfortable she felt in his presence. Granted, they were far from strangers, yet they had never been in the position of actually being out with each other, and she was surprised at how relaxed and natural she felt with him.

And strangely enough, he seemed to feel the same way.

Before they knew it, the dinner had been consumed, and two hours later they were still lingering over yet another pot of tea.

The conversation ranged from politics to their childhoods and even to old love affairs. Since Zack already knew about Skip, Toni found herself relating some of the good times that had occurred during that time of her life. Zack listened with interest, wondering just how much in love she still was with Skip Harden. She talked as if the affair were over and forgotten, yet there was a wistful, almost sad light shining in her eyes when she said his name.

The man had hurt her, there was no doubt about that, but was she really over him? Somehow, Zack felt she wasn't, and for some reason that bothered him.

"He really did a job on you, didn't he?" he sympathized when Toni went into more detail of her recent breakup.

"I guess so, but I'll survive."

"I know you will, but have you ever considered talking to someone about the breakup? Sometimes it can really help a person to get it all out in the open."

She was afraid he would think she was talking too much about her problem. "I have. I'm talking to you," she reasoned.

"No, I mean someone professional."

There was a small, almost imperceptible movement on her part as she tensed involuntarily with resentment. "Are you suggesting I should see a doctor?" she asked coolly.

Now this was really too much. She liked him, a lot, but she felt he might be overstepping his bounds just a little. She could understand his not believing about the flying saucer, and he had caught her in some pretty compromising situations since they had met, but to suggest that there was something actually wrong with her? No way.

"Well, I don't know. I just thought maybe all this upheaval in your life has been too much of an emotional stress on you," he hedged. "That's certainly nothing to be ashamed of. Life has a way of hitting us in the gut when we least suspect it, and it's only reasonable to ask for help at those times."

"Have I done something to suggest to you that I'm not able to handle my stress?" she prodded in the same glacial tone as before.

"No. I mean, yes. Take the flying saucer, for instance."

"I saw it."

"Yes, I know you thought you did."

"I did."

"I thought you admitted yourself that you weren't sure that's what it was," he shot back.

"I wasn't at first, but the more I think about it, the more certain I am of what I saw. You may not believe in flying saucers, but don't try to tell me I didn't see one."

"Okay, okay, so you did. Maybe. But I still don't think it would hurt for you to talk to someone. Now, I have a good friend—"

"Just exactly what are you trying to say, Zack? That I'm a real flake and should be locked up somewhere?"

"No, you're not a flake." He said the words as if he were trying to convince himself, not her, that she was perfectly sane. "Maybe you're just confused right now and *thought* you saw something . . . unusual," he suggested patiently. "That's not surprising for a person who has suffered a traumatic experience such as you have. That's why I think you should seek some professional help before it goes any further."

"Look, don't worry about me, okay? I appreciate your concern, but we obviously don't see eye to eye about the existence of flying saucers." Toni decided to change the subject before they ended up in a big argument. Besides, she felt as if she had been dominating the floor all evening with the boring details of her problems, and she really wanted to know more about him. "What about you, Mr. Sane and completely normal Tremayne? Any lost loves you're mourning over?" She knew he had told her once before there wasn't, but she was just testing.

Zack gave up trying to talk any sense into her and pitched his napkin up on the table in defeat. Obviously she was not open to any suggestions about the improvement of her mental state at the moment. "None at all."

"That figures, but it's disgusting just the same," Toni grumbled. "Everyone should have their heart ripped out once just so they can be accused of being nuts and seeing flying saucers." She grinned quickly to show she was only teasing. "Right?"

"Having my heart ripped out is one thing I've tried to avoid," Zack grumbled, still a little put out at her because she wouldn't let him help.

"You've never been in love before?"

"Only once, and she was an older woman."

"Aha! You told me once you had never been in love with another woman. Remember? The night we were sitting in my swing and—"

"I know, I know, but I had forgotten about Miss Margarite Perriwrinkle. She was my kind of woman: tall, leggy, hair the color of corn silk, and the prettiest blue eyes I've ever seen." He sighed. "But, she was convinced that there was too much difference in our age and the love affair would never work."

"How sad. How many years' difference was it?"

"Forty. She was my second-grade teacher."

"Oh, poor Zackery. That must have been crushing," Toni sympathized with a contrived but appropriately woeful expression on her face. "Some women just have no heart whatsoever."

"I know, and it was crushing. It took me almost a week to pull out of my depression and ask Patty Wilcox to carry the bats outside for me at recess again."

"And no doubt she did?"

"Oh, sure. I was unusually charming for a man of seven, and she couldn't resist. She even offered to be third base for me."

"You mean she offered to play third base for you?"

"No." He sighed heavily again. "She wanted to

be third base. I'm telling you, I had it back then, and it was hard to ignore."

She eyed him warily. He had it *now,* and he knew it. "I'll bet; but what about Karol?"

"What about her?"

"Well, I mean, living right next door to you, I can't help but notice you seemed to, shall I say, favor Ms. Massenburg's company more than the rest of your entourage."

"Tsk tsk, Ms. Cameron." He lifted his brow distastefully. "Could I perchance have yet another nosy neighbor?"

"No, I'm not nosy," she denied. "But you have to admit that your social calendar is never lacking for attention, and your front door is usually flapping like a broken shutter in a high wind from the women running in and out of your house."

He shrugged dramatically. "I guess I haven't changed that much from when I was seven." He had to duck quickly to keep from getting hit as she pitched her napkin at him in exasperation.

"Okay, Ms. Busybody. Karol Massenburg and I are just friends. That's all."

"That's not what I hear." Toni couldn't resist in a singsong voice.

"I'm aware of the rumors at the courthouse concerning my intentions toward Karol, but until they are confirmed by me, don't believe a word you hear." His tone suddenly turned very serious as he picked up his teacup and took another sip.

"I wouldn't dream of it."

"And stop watching my front door"—he winked at her solemnly—"and I'll stop watching yours."

"If you're watching mine, you'll die of boredom," she warned, yet she couldn't help but feel an unexpected thrill shoot through her at his admission that he had been taking note of what she was doing, too.

"Yeah, well, I had noticed you were not exactly a social butterfly."

"Believe me, I'm not even a gregarious moth," she murmured glumly.

The hour was growing late as they finally finished their last pot of tea and left the restaurant. Toni insisted on paying the bill, and even though she could tell it annoyed Zack, he permitted it.

"After all, I was the one who invited you," she shouted as they ran to her car in the midst of another downpour.

"Maybe so, but you're the first woman in my life whom I have ever let take me out," he shouted back as they reached the car and he held the passenger side door open for her.

"Don't you want me to drive?"

"No!" He closed the door and raced around the side of her car and got in. "From now on, me man and you woman. Got it?"

"Do your women not drive cars?"

"Not when they're with me. It's an old custom that started with my grandfather. Okay?"

"Okay."

The drive home was pleasant, with the wipers slapping gently in a hypnotic rhythm across the rain-covered windshield. They both hummed along softly with a popular ballad that was playing on the radio.

All too soon, Zack was turning onto her driveway, and she found herself wishing the evening had been longer.

"Okay." Zack killed the engine and turned to face her with an exaggerated sigh. "What's next?"

"What do you mean, what's next?"

"Well, like I said earlier, I've never had a woman take me out, so I don't know what to expect."

"What do *you* think happens next?"

"I'm afraid it's decision time," he said in mock frustration. "Undoubtedly, you're going to want to kiss me and I'll have to ask myself, 'Do I take the chance on letting her kiss me good night on our first date and hope she won't think I'm easy, or do I hold out until we get to know each other better?' "

"Decisions, decisions. Always decisions," she agreed with a hopeless sigh herself. "And then there *is* always the risk I'll think you're loose."

"Yeah, then there's always the risk I'll reveal how loose I really am." He looked at her and wiggled his brows playfully.

"You *said* you were a gentleman."

"I said that?" he asked incredulously.

"That's right."

"A momentary lapse of—something or other, I can assure you."

"Then perhaps I should just play it safe and give you a very sisterly kiss and make a quick departure."

"Good idea. I think we'll be safe that way." He reached over and gently pulled her to him. "Now, don't scare me," he warned. "I'm not very experienced."

She nearly choked on that one.

"I can see that. I'll try to be gentle." Reaching up to wind her arms around his neck, she pulled their faces close together, and the scent of his aftershave made her tingle with longing. The kiss they had shared on the swing had left her weak in the knees, so why was she deliberately walking into this one? She was playing with fire tonight, and she knew it. Already the desire that she had been pushing aside for the past few weeks was coming achingly alive, and warning bells were going off in her head as he drew her nearer.

Careful, Toni. This is only a harmless little kiss, one he will take much more lightly than you will.

She closed her eyes for a moment and savored his wonderful scent as he drew her flush against him. He felt warm and very comforting to her.

"Go ahead, Ms. Cameron," he teased in a husky tone, "Make my day."

Their mouths closed over one another's—gently at first, then with growing enthusiasm. At first he seemed a little surprised at the intensity with which she threw herself into the embrace, but moments later he found himself drowning in the warmth of her womanly softness.

Toni hated to admit how much she had missed this part of her life, and she was terribly afraid he would arrive at the wrong conclusion if she continued to clasp on to him like a love-starved animal the way she was; but as the kiss deepened and grew hungry, almost frantic, she felt herself throwing caution to the wind and kissing him back with a fervor that surely astounded him.

Shifting around in the seat with a muffled groan,

Zack took the initiative this time, and he kissed her with mastery that left her weak with desire. One kiss turned into two, two into three, and suddenly she found herself clinging to him helplessly as their mouths met time and time again. White-hot fire shot through her veins, and she couldn't believe she was responding to him as she was. Even at the height of passion, she had never reacted to Skip's kisses in the way she was to Zack's.

And it wasn't only Toni who had unexpectedly lost control of her emotions. Strangely, Zack seemed to have lost control of his, also.

Within a few moments they were both breathless with desire.

"Toni . . . honey. I don't know about this," Zack groaned again as she brought his mouth back to meet hers in a searing kiss.

She had no idea what had gotten into her, but suddenly she wanted—and needed—him desperately.

Somehow, Zack had the wisdom to realize what was happening.

An average man would have quickly taken advantage of the situation and whispered a sexy invitation to her to adjourn to the bedroom.

Her hunger was a tangible thing, and he knew she wanted him in this dramatic flare of passion as badly as he wanted her. It would be so easy to take her, to hold her in his arms and make love to her and completely forget the fact that she had been deeply hurt by another man who had once felt the same mind-boggling desire for her but had no thoughts for what their relationship would be in the light of morning when the fire had finally died down.

Yes, so very, very easy—she was soft and sweet and all woman. But he couldn't do that to her.

Instead, he very gently broke away from her, realizing that what she was feeling was the culmination of long-denied sexual tension, and that if he lightly took from her what she in her momentary confusion would give, he would later regret this night. Maybe with someone else he would have, but not with her. And he was powerless to understand why.

"You're a very tempting lady," he murmured as he placed gentle, featherlike kisses along the side of her face. "But I think we'd better break this up."

For just a moment, Toni was hurt by his rejection; then the impact of his words hit home. She had once more almost let her emotions overrule her common sense.

What she was feeling was the natural reaction of a woman who had once enjoyed a very fulfilling sex life and was now without one, and wisely Zack had sensed that. Her feelings had nothing to do with him, and even if they did, it was plain that he was not interested in starting a relationship with her.

She should have known that. His type didn't want permanence, and she knew that in the long run she would never again settle for anything less.

To her mortification, a burst of tension-relieving giggles broke out as she scooted guiltily away from him. "Yes, you're right," she snickered, then swiftly clapped her hand over her mouth in mortification. Oh, please, she couldn't start giggling now!

He edged away a fraction and looked at her oddly.

"I'm sorry. When I get nervous, I—" she snickered, then buried her face in her hands helplessly.

What must he think of her sitting here laughing like an idiot when he had just refused to make love to her!

"Are you all right?"

"Yes."

Well, it was plain to see that she wasn't all right, but he had no idea what to do about it.

"What's so funny?" he frowned worriedly. Good Lord, he wished he could figure her out. She seemed perfectly sane most of the time, but then she had *these* times.

"Nothing." As quickly as the giggles had started, they rapidly disappeared, and she straightened herself up and dabbed at her watery eyes. She was really going to have to do something about this annoying affliction.

He waited for a moment while she pulled herself together; then he gently reached out and tipped her face up to meet his. "Are you sure you're all right?"

"Yes, I'm fine—really." Another burst of laughter escaped before she quickly put a lid on it. "Well, I guess I'll go in. It's getting late," she announced in a perfectly normal voice.

Reaching for the handle on the door, she was about to open it when he stopped her. "Toni, at least think about what we discussed earlier."

"Seeing a doctor?" Of course, he *would* think she was a little touched after the display she had just put on, but she knew she was as normal as sunshine. "I don't think so, Zack."

She had no intention of seeing a doctor. She was perfectly all right, except for this minor little annoyance.

"Hey, are you mad at me?" He raised her face back to meet his. He couldn't tell if he had offended her or not, but he certainly hadn't meant to. It was as hard on him to break off their lovemaking as it had been for her.

She decided then not to keep beating around the bush and to let him know she was getting a little tired of him implying there was something mentally wrong with her. "Yes, I *am* mad, Zackery. I *do* giggle when I get nervous, I *may* do a few odd things on occasion, and I *did* see the flying saucer in your backyard, but I'm *not* nuts!"

"Toni, honey. I don't know what to do when you get like this!"

She opened the car door and quickly slid out. "Don't worry, Zack. I won't start foaming at the mouth." She slammed the door loudly and marched up her walk in the rain.

The rat fink! He not only didn't want to get involved with her, he thought she was a mental case!

Well, fine! She didn't like him either!

And even if she did, never again would she let herself become emotionally dependent upon a man, and tonight had served as a good warning to her. No matter how attractive Zackery Tremayne happened to be, he definitely wasn't the man she was looking for in her life.

In fact, she was beginning to think he was nothing but a Skip clone, and that made her stomach more than a little queasy.

Men. Who needed them, anyway?

CHAPTER SEVEN

Well, Zack may think she was a little off, but there was one thing she was absolutely sure of.

That pesky goat was in her yard again.

Toni stood at her window the following weekend and watched the uninvited guest reach up with its mouth and jerk a pair of her newest panties off the clothesline and proceed to munch away on them.

She had no idea how the goat had gotten over the fence again, but it had been nothing but a nuisance to her for the last week.

Throwing the door open, she shouted at the animal to stop its assault on her wardrobe, but by now the panties were a mangled mess.

The goat looked up from his position on the lawn and seemed to decide that although there was a lot of commotion going on, he actually was in no immediate danger. He reached up and jerked her new bra off the line and proceeded to devour it, too.

That was the limit. She had just bought those new underthings, and he was calmly standing there chewing up thirty dollars of her hard-earned money without so much as blinking an eye!

Rushing down the back steps, she waved her

hands wildly and demanded again that he stop it this minute!

Zack was standing in his kitchen, and at the sound of her high-pitched voice, his head snapped up expectantly. Toni was rushing out her back door waving her arms wildly in the air and yelling at the top of her lungs for someone to stop something. He stood on tiptoe and tried to see what she was upset about, but he could find nothing unusual taking place. The goat was well hidden behind the wooden fence, so he had no idea what she was after. He shook his head and calmly went back to mixing up his homemade spaghetti sauce.

That woman had a problem.

The goat jumped and backed away as Toni flew out the door at him; he realized that he had pushed his luck too far.

It was plain to see, even for a goat, that she was in a real snit this time.

The animal bolted and tried to jump the fence that he had come over a few minutes earlier, but he quickly decided that the woman was quicker than she used to be.

Before he knew what was happening to him, she had nabbed him by the tail and was hanging on for dear life while he nearly choked on the bits of bra still hanging out of his mouth.

"I have had it with you!" she screeched angrily. *"This* time, I'm going to call your owners and demand restitution for your despicable lack of manners!"

Ordinarily, she would have been a little more patient in a case like this, but this was not the goat's first offense.

Oh, no. Not by a long shot.

Twice before, she had caught him pillaging her laundry, but at that time she had had no idea who he belonged to. Since then, she had made it her business to find out who owned the little crumbsnatcher, and this time he wasn't going to get away with it.

Dragging the goat by the collar, she manhandled him up the steps and into her kitchen. She wasn't about to give him the opportunity to break away from her. She would bring him into the house with her where she could keep a close eye on him while she phoned the owners.

The goat put up a pretty fair fight, but in the end he realized that she had overpowered him, so he settled down docilely as she slipped a rope through his collar and tied him to the oven door handle.

"There. See if you can chew your way out of that," she challenged smugly.

The goat looked extremely guilty and studiously tried to avoid her eyes. She could almost have felt sorry for him if it were not for the fact that he still had remnants of lace from her bra clinging to his beard.

Snapping open a drawer, she withdrew the phone directory and began to search for the number of the animal's owner, Morgan Dooley on Willow Drive, still mumbling heatedly under her breath about people who didn't take care of their pets.

As she turned her back and began to punch out the digits, the goat managed to get the cabinet door open and pull out a box of cornflakes.

115

"I'd like to speak to Mr. Morgan Dooley, please!" she demanded as a voice came on the line.

Two sharp raps sounded on the back door, and Toni recognized Zack's knock. She waited for Mr. Dooley to come to the phone.

"Come in!" He probably wanted to borrow something again, she thought as she glanced over irritably at the goat, who was crunching loudly on the box of cold cereal.

That's right! Make yourself right at home! She seethed and proceeded to shoot murderous glares in the animal's direction.

"Hi." Zack stuck his head around the door. "I'm right in the middle of making spaghetti sauce, and I just discovered I'm out of tomato sauce. . . ." His voice trailed off lamely as his eyes fastened on the goat.

"Second cabinet on the left," Toni muttered, then quickly returned her attention to her call. "Yes, I can wait."

Mr. Dooley was apparently out cutting his lawn instead of minding his goat, as he was supposed to be doing.

Well, he would soon be getting his goat, or she would be getting his! She turned and faced the window, her eyes grimly surveying what little of her wash was still flapping on the line.

Stepping hesitantly into the kitchen, Zack cautiously tiptoed around the goat, who looked him over carefully but didn't let his unexpected appearance interrupt his snack. He dipped into the box for another huge bite and munched away.

Zack opened the cabinet door and fumbled

around, quickly locating a can of tomato sauce, all the while keeping a close eye on the animal tied to the kitchen stove. When he found what he had come for, he edged back slowly to the door.

"Find what you needed?" Toni called over her shoulder.

"Yeah, thanks."

"No problem."

Moments later, Zack stepped across the hedge, then stopped and glanced back over his shoulder suspiciously.

Was there actually a goat in her kitchen eating cornflakes?

He frowned. Nah. No way.

He was getting to be as crazy as she was.

Later, after seeing Morgan Dooley and his recalcitrant goat out, Toni closed the door and her attention was drawn to the light burning in Zack's kitchen.

He and Karol were probably eating by now, she thought with a whimsical sigh. That is, she assumed it was Karol he was entertaining again tonight.

Well, he wouldn't have to worry about her butting in on them as she had last time. It was clear that Zackery Tremayne didn't care for lowly stenographers who imagined they saw flying saucers, specifically, flying saucers that were trying to steal his barbecue grill. He clearly preferred the more intellectual type like Karol, even though *she* believed in their existence, too, and he didn't think she was cuckoo.

Since meeting Karol Massenburg, Toni had found

out through the grapevine at work that not only was she a judge herself, but her father was a very influential and prominent pillar of the community.

It was rumored that Karol had her sights set for Zackery Tremayne, and her father, Judge Theodore Massenburg, had big plans for his future, so she guessed that that sort of ruled out any new romantic interests on Zack's part.

And even if Karol weren't in the picture, Toni had to admit that she herself had not always presented her best side in Zack's presence. It seemed he was forever catching her doing crazy things.

Take the other night, for instance. She had hurried home from work, utterly miserable from a kink she had endured all day in her shoulder and neck. The only thing she could figure out was that she had slept on her arm wrong the night before, so that when she had awakened that morning, it was stiff and sore.

She had managed to work all day, but when she arrived home, she had hurriedly stripped off her jacket and begun to try to work the pain out of her sore joints. In her haste for relief, she had left the front door standing wide open, and she was just in the process of swinging her arm around and around in big, wide circles, groaning with agony, when she glanced up. And who should she see standing there watching her with a puzzled expression on his face, but Zack Tremayne!

She had grinned at him weakly as she felt her heart sink to the floor.

But instead of simply explaining about her arm, she was too embarrassed about her seemingly questionable behavior, so like an idiot she decided to not say anything, hoping that perhaps he hadn't noticed.

Instead, she had quickly thanked him for bringing her evening paper to her and hurriedly slammed the door in his face.

And to top that off, only a few days later, he had come over to return the hose he had borrowed, and he had caught her talking and laughing to herself in the kitchen like a blubbering imbecile.

She had been scraping carrots to cook for dinner when a funny incident that had happened at work that day had popped in her mind. Before she knew it, she was reliving the incident, chuckling out loud and saying ridiculous things like "I couldn't believe it!" and "Poor Rita!"

Since she had been living alone, she had found herself talking out loud more than once. She had tried to break the habit, always reasoning that one of these days someone was going to overhear her and think she was completely nuts!

Well, that day had arrived, and she was embarrassed to tears that *he* had been the one to catch her. But again, she decided to ignore what she had been doing in the faint hope that she wasn't losing her mind and he hadn't actually heard her giggling like a deranged hyena.

After all, her mother had talked to herself for years, and she wasn't crazy.

And now, of all the rotten luck, he had caught her with a goat in her kitchen, and he still hadn't said a word.

119

Could she even dare to hope that he had missed that, too?

Of course not. Granted, he was extremely nice, but he wasn't blind.

And then, of course, there had been the incident the other night when she had made a complete fool of herself by laughing in his face when he had called a halt to their heated necking.

If he had left it up to her, she shuddered to think what might have happened.

The thought of his kisses sent her blood racing once more, and she had to admit that although he was a pain sometimes, he was certainly all man at others.

At times, she worried that she was growing closer to him than was wise. Although they were good friends, she knew that Zack would probably be the last man alive, with the exception of Skip, who wanted any sort of permanent commitment. Yet there wasn't a day that went by that he didn't stop by her house, or she his.

Last night she had been sitting out in her swing when he came home around eleven. There had been a brief thunder shower earlier in the evening, and the smell of the freshly dampened earth was pleasantly in the air.

Zack got out of his car and glanced over at her house, as he usually did.

"Hi!" she called softly.

"Hi. You still up?"

"Uh-huh. You're in early tonight."

He stepped over the hedge and walked over to prop his hands on the porch railing behind the swing. "Yeah, Mom, you can go to bed now." He grinned.

"I wasn't waiting up for you," she denied, but she had been. She always slept better when she knew he was safely tucked away in his own bed.

"What did you do tonight?" He slipped around the porch and took his place on the swing next to her.

For a moment she felt a little embarrassed that he had caught her in her nightgown again. "Not much. Washed my hair and gave myself a manicure."

Zack lifted up one of her hands to admire her handiwork. "They look good."

"Thank you. I'm glad you approve."

Their eyes met and lingered for a moment before she asked in a conspiratorial whisper, "And what exciting thing did you do tonight, Mr. Tremayne?"

"Sat in a stuffy old meeting with six other judges until I thought I was going to nod off on them." She noticed that he was still holding her hand, and she made no effort to retrieve it. "I was glad when it finally broke up."

In a gesture so natural that neither one noticed, Zack's arm went around her, and she laid her head on his shoulder. They sat in silence for a few moments, swinging back and forth, content to share the peaceful time together.

Even though there was a faint trace of cigarette smoke lingering on his clothes, she could still smell his aftershave, and it caused her pulse to race a little faster.

"I like your aftershave," she admitted.

He glanced down at her, grinning. "You do?"

121

"Yeah, it's nice."

"Want to taste it?" he bantered. "I think there may be a trace still left along in through here." He pointed to a spot just at the corner of his mouth.

"Are you sure you wouldn't mind?" she bantered back. "If it tastes as good as it smells, I may go buy a bottle just to snack on."

"No need to do that," he discouraged her, easing her closer to his descending mouth. "You can borrow mine any time you want." And once again they were kissing.

At first they were light, playful pecks; then she settled into his arms, and his mouth hungrily took hers. They exchanged kiss after smoldering kiss, and before long they were both aroused past the point of clear thinking.

"I don't know about you," Zack murmured against her mouth as their tongues teased one another's. She was beginning to worry him. With her he felt something totally different from what he felt with other women. She could send his blood boiling by a mere flick of those blue eyes in his direction. And yet he was reluctant to start anything with her. Somehow he felt that if he did make love to her, he would want more—and he wasn't at all sure he was ready for that sort of commitment in his life yet.

"You know more about me than most people do," she said as she kissed his eyes and then his nose and then, with a soft sigh, went back to his mouth.

"Maybe. But you confuse me."

It would have been the proper time to explore his strange statement, but her heart told her there were more important things to do.

Zack was here in her arms, and for the moment everything was right in her world.

Yet Zack continued to keep his distance, even though she had carefully refrained from bringing up the subject of flying saucers in his presence again.

That touchy subject, coupled with the incriminating circumstances he had caught her in recently, made her wonder if he didn't really think she was a little bit bonkers.

Still, she couldn't help but wonder why, in all the weeks she had lived next door to him, he had never once shown any sign of recognizing the fact that she was not only his neighbor but a single woman, completely devoid of male companionship at the moment, *perfectly* capable of accepting a real date with him if he should ever care to ask. But no, *she* had been the one to ask him for the one and only official date they had ever had, and that date had turned out to be less than satisfactory.

She would have thought that, considering his humming social life, just *once* he would be curious enough to invite her out for an evening, but so far he hadn't.

She could only assume it was because of his relationship with Karol. And yet he didn't seem the type to go out with a woman, then return home to steal a kiss from his neighbor.

Yes, she had to admit, Zackery was truly becoming a puzzle to her.

She supposed that most women coming out of the situation she had just come out of would be turned off by men for a while. But strangely enough, she wasn't.

What she and Skip had had together could have been really wonderful if they had entered into marriage to begin with instead of a live-in relationship. True, a legal document did not necessarily assure a happy future, but it seemed to her that there would be more of a commitment, more of a serious binding of two souls, when it was done that way and vows were exchanged.

Yes, she knew there could be joy in the right relationship with the right man, and she was even willing to risk the chance of being hurt again if it meant finding that one right person.

She glanced at the house next door and sighed again. Wouldn't it be something if that right person was living right next door to her?

She quickly cast away the winsome thought. He didn't seem to know she existed other than as his eccentric neighbor.

And by golly, she would rather give up her styling mousse—forever!—before she asked him out again!

"Are you trying to say you think she's a fruitcake?" Jim Howerton glanced up from behind his desk and grinned devilishly at Zack.

"Not a fruitcake—necessarily. I'm just a little worried about her." Zack rose from the chair he had been sitting in and went to look out the window behind Jim's massive oak desk. He could see almost the entire city from where he stood, and he studied the buildings scattered below him thoughtfully.

"You know, I've known her for weeks now, and we've become good friends."

"Now, come on, Zack. Don't try to kid an ol' kidder," Jim teased as he leaned back in his chair and propped his feet up on his desk. "Just friends?"

"That's right, just friends," he stated firmly. "There's nothing going on between us. I just feel sort of responsible for her, that's all."

That wasn't entirely true. She had been in his thoughts lately more than he cared to admit. He supposed this uncharacteristic protectiveness he felt for her was due to the fact that he knew she didn't have anyone else to look after her. At times, he had to wonder if she could take care of herself.

No, that wasn't true, either. In all fairness, she did a pretty good job of taking care of herself, especially since, until recently, she had had someone to help her share her life and solve her problems. He guessed she had the right to act a little screwy after what she had been through with Skip Harden.

The guy must be an idiot to have given her up, he thought, surprised that he should feel a little envious of Toni's previous boyfriend.

No, when it came right down to it, Toni Cameron was a survivor. She would make it on her own, and he had to admit that he admired her spirit to overcome her disappointments and get on with life.

Not to mention her legs. She still had the best set of legs that he had ever seen.

And he had to admit, each time he had been with her lately had left him pretty shaken. Yet there were also times when he had caught her acting weird, and that was what had brought him here today.

"You're sure you're just friends? She's a foxy-lookin' chick," Jim pursued with a mischievous grin.

"I'm positive." But she was sharp, he couldn't deny that, he added silently.

"How's Karol?" Jim abruptly changed the subject as he reached for a piece of peppermint candy that he kept in a dish on his desk.

"Karol's fine."

Popping the candy into his mouth, Jim contemplated Zack thoughtfully. "I figured you two would be engaged by now."

Zack laughed. "Well, you along with all the other busybodies figured wrong."

"Now wait a minute," Jim protested. "You have to admit, you've been seeing her pretty steadily lately, and the fact that her father could set you up on easy street should make you stop and think about the possibilities there. You could do a whole lot worse."

"I don't choose a woman by what she can do for me, any more than you do," Zack replied. "Karol is a lovely lady, and it isn't any secret that I have the utmost respect for Ted Massenburg, but as far as marriage between Karol and me is concerned, that's out of the question. In fact, we had a long talk last night, and we decided we aren't going to see each other as regularly as we have been. I'm just not ready for that sort of commitment to her right now, and I think she understands that."

Jim's dubious "harrumph" annoyed Zack. "What's the 'harrumph' for?"

126

"Nothing, it was just a harmless little 'harrumph.'"

"Well, stuff your 'harrumphs,' and do me a little favor."

"Name it, ol' buddy, and it's yours."

"Ask Toni out on a date."

"I already have, twice. She won't go out with me." Jim had an irritating smirk on his face as Zack turned around slowly to look at him.

"You've already asked her out?" The swift stab of jealousy that immediately shot through him at Jim's announcement took him totally by surprise. He couldn't remember ever feeling so resentful of another man where a woman was concerned. "When?"

"Oh, just couple of times," he replied evasively. "Why?"

"No reason. I'm just a little surprised, that's all." His eyes turned darkly suspicious.

"I don't know why that would surprise you," Jim reasoned uneasily, aware of the tension that had suddenly cropped up between them. "You just said you weren't interested in her."

"No—no I'm not." Zack managed to pull himself together and turn his gaze back to the window. "I just didn't think about you asking her out."

"Well, it doesn't matter. I've asked her, and she always has some sort of excuse why she can't go out with me," Jim said with a defeated sigh.

"Then we're going to have to think of a way to make her accept."

It was Jim who looked suspicious now. "I had the distinct impression that you weren't too happy

127

about the idea of her going out with me." In his opinion, Zack was not making an ounce of sense. First he wanted him to ask Toni out, then he acted resentful when he told him he already had.

"Nonsense. I don't care whether she goes out with you or not," he lied. "In fact, I want her to, so you can question her and see if you think her problems are getting too serious for her to handle. When I try to suggest she might need a little help, she gets mad at me."

Jim let out a low whistle. "You really think she's gone bonkers?"

"No, I don't think she's bonkers, but then, I'm not the doctor. You are."

"Yeah, maybe so, but what makes you think she'll talk to me?"

"Because as far as I know, she doesn't realize you're a psychiatrist, does she?"

"I haven't mentioned it."

"Good. Then you can question her without raising her suspicions."

"About what?"

Zack began to pace the floor agitatedly. "Well, for starters, ask her about the flying saucers she's seen in my backyard, about the goat in her kitchen, about the way I catch her talking to herself and swinging her arms around in the air, not to mention the way she runs out her back door occasionally screaming at the top of her lungs; and *if* she manages to come up with a satisfactory answer to those questions, then you might find out why she sits and giggles like an idiot for no apparent reason at all when a man has refused to let things . . . get out of hand."

"Oh no! Nothing going on between the two of you, huh?" Jim quickly seized upon Zack's slip of the tongue.

"No, there isn't! It was just a friendly kiss—or at least it started off that way, and when it started getting out of hand, I decided we were neither one ready for that sort of thing yet, so I called a halt, and you know what she did?"

He paused and looked at Jim irritably.

"No, what?" Jim absently crunched down on his mint as he became caught up in the conversation.

"She laughed in my face!"

"No kidding." He let out a low whistle.

"She did. And she swears she's seen a flying saucer in my backyard, and when I suggest that she get some professional help, she gets all bent out of shape."

"What makes you think she didn't see one?"

Zack groaned in exasperation. "Don't tell me *you* believe those cock-and-bull stories about flying saucers, too!"

"Well, I don't know if I do or not. I've heard some pretty fascinating tales on the subject. Who knows? There might be something out there that we don't know about."

"Well, that isn't the case here. Toni just happens to have come out of a relationship that hurt her very much, and I think her mind's just playing tricks on her. That's why I want you to talk to her."

"You don't think she would let me help her if she knew that I'm a doctor?"

"If she finds out you're a doctor, we're both in hot water," Zack warned. "So be careful, Howerton, and don't blow it. Just talk to her, and then tell me what you think I should do to help her."

"I don't think it will ever work, and I'm highly opposed to such unethical and underhanded methods."

"But I've done you a lot of favors, so you'll swallow your morality and help me this time, won't you?" Zack finished for him.

Jim sighed defeatedly. "I will, but I'm against it."

"Thanks. I'll owe you one."

"No thanks needed. I'll collect from Toni—personally," he quipped with a knowing wiggle of his brows. Going out with Toni Cameron was not exactly his idea of punishment.

The scowl on Zack's face told him he didn't find his remark funny.

"Only kidding."

"Just see that you keep your hands to yourself while you're with her."

As old college buddies, Zack knew Jim could come on pretty strong when it came to women, and he was beginning to doubt the wisdom of asking him to take Toni out. Maybe he should have arranged their meeting when *he* could be there to see what went on.

"Yes, Daddy. I'll be good," Jim said mockingly.

"I mean it, Jim."

"Okay, okay. I'll be a real saint."

Zack's grin widened. "You'd better be."

"If you're that worried about my behavior, then maybe we should make it a double date."

"No, I don't think that would be a good idea. I want you to take Toni somewhere where you can talk to her in private, but I just don't want you getting out of line with her. Understand?"

"Yes, sir. I can tell you're not interested in her in the least."

"I'm not—at least not like you're thinking. I'm just not going to throw her to a wolf." Zack grinned.

"Well, whatever you say. But listen, if you're free tonight, why don't I drop by and you can fix me one of your terrific steaks for all the trouble I'm going to for you?"

"I can't fix you a steak."

"Why not?"

"Because"—Zack cleared his throat nervously and glanced back out the window—"somebody stole my grill."

"Stole it?"

"Yes, stole it!" Zack's expression became defensive. "One of those neighborhood hoodlums I see running around must have taken it."

But he really didn't know *who* had taken the grill. It had simply been gone one morning this week when he had walked out to get in his car to go to work. Needless to say, he wasn't about to tell Jim where Toni would insist it had gone. He would think they were both nuts.

"Too bad. Did you report it to the police?"

"Of course I did, but I haven't heard anything yet."

"Well, you'll probably get it back. It's a pretty

distinct-looking piece of property," Jim said comfortingly.

"Yeah." Zack glanced cautiously up at the sky. "I sure hope so."

CHAPTER EIGHT

She knew it! She knew she should have gotten the soft contact lenses instead of the hard ones, but it was too late now. She would just have to suffer through these until she could get used to them. She blinked hard and tried to see through the stream of tears as she sat in Poocie's, one of the nicer restaurants in town, and waited for Jim Howerton to join her.

When he called last night and invited her to have dinner with him, her first inclination had been to make up some excuse why she couldn't, but she quickly discarded the tempting thought.

She had done that twice already, and she didn't want to hurt his feelings. It wasn't that she didn't like him; it was just that he held no particular appeal to her. And she *had* been busy.

She blinked hard again and dabbed miserably at her tears with a handkerchief. It felt as if she had a giant prickly cactus in her eyes.

Her vision was so bad, she wasn't even aware that Jim had arrived until she heard the voice of the waiter seating him at her table.

Squinting her eyes to try to make out his features, she smiled and blinked hard again. "Hi there!"

"Hello. Sorry I'm running a little late, but I got tied up at work."

Jim smiled back at her uncertainly as she blinked forcefully and widened her eyes in an attempt to clear her eyesight.

"Oh, that's all right. I haven't been here very long myself."

He cleared his throat nervously, then glanced down at the menu, trying to ignore her rather strange behavior. It would be too much to hope that she was trying to flirt with him and botching the attempt. No, Zack may be right. She may need his services even more than he had thought.

The waiter returned and took their drink order. When he left, Jim turned his attention back to her. "Well, well. So how have you been?"

Apparently not so hot. Her eyes were red and weepy, and she looked downright miserable.

"Really good, thank you. And you?"

"Fine, fine."

They grinned self-consciously at each other and she blinked three times in rapid succession. She knew he had to be wondering what her problem was, so she decided to fill him in. "My eyes have been bothering me a little."

"Yes, I can see that. Have you had them checked lately?" Jim inquired in a concerned voice.

She sighed. "Yes, but the doctor said I'd just have to get used to them."

Jim looked blank for a moment. Get used to what? Her eyes? "Yes. Well . . ." He snapped the

134

menu back open and pretended to study the entrees while he planned his strategy. Zack was definitely right. She had some problems. "What looks good?"

She tried to make out the small print blurring before her and couldn't. "I'm afraid I can't read," she apologized. She primly folded up the menu and laid it back on the table. "I'll just have what you have."

He lowered his menu a fraction. Was she illiterate, too? "Uh, well, sure. I've heard the prime rib is excellent here."

"That sounds lovely. I like mine medium-well."

When the waiter returned, Jim ordered for both of them as Toni fumbled around in her purse to retrieve a small bottle of solution. While his attention was diverted, she swiftly scrunched down behind the tablecloth and put a drop in her left eye.

Jim finished the order and glanced down at her. "Are you all right?"

She grinned at him sheepishly as she quickly slid back up in her chair. "Fine, thank you."

They sat in silence for a moment, glancing idly around the crowded room. Toni frantically searched her mind for a topic of conversation but could think of nothing.

"So." Jim folded his hands on the table and smiled at her. "Have you seen Zack lately?"

She sat up straighter, relieved that he had found something to talk about.

"Oh, I see him going in and out every day, but I haven't talked to him recently."

"I understand you two work together on occasion."

"Yes, occasionally."

"What do you do?"

"I'm a stenographer."

An illiterate stenographer! How strange.

For the next few minutes, Jim chatted amiably about this and that until he sensed that she was beginning to feel at ease with him. Then, very smoothly, he began to bring up various subjects that she found very strange that he would want to discuss on a first date.

"What about your childhood? Did you have a happy one?"

"Well, it wasn't unhappy," she replied. "I guess you could say it was a very normal one."

"Do you have brothers and sisters?"

"No, I'm an only child. Do you?"

"Uh, yes. I have a brother."

"That's nice. Was your childhood a happy one?"

"Not really."

"Oh, what a shame. Was it due to your parents?"

Jim's face grew resentful. "No, my parents were fine. It was my brother who caused all the problems. We were always competing with each other."

His voice had suddenly turned a little sulky, she thought.

"Oh, sibling rivalry." Toni nodded her head sympathetically. "That can be tough. Would you like to talk about it?" She knew it helped sometimes to have someone to open up to, and Jim looked absolutely miserable at the mention of his brother.

"Well, actually . . ." Before he knew what he was doing, Jim was confiding in Toni about his feelings of insecurity while growing up. For the next half hour, he droned on and on about the injustices —imaginary or real, Toni couldn't quite decide— that he had suffered because of his brother, until she was almost sorry she had offered a sympathetic ear.

But Jim was delighted to find someone who listened so attentively to *his* problems for a change. He found Toni to be a good listener and surprisingly astute about how he should deal with his problem. This was a woman he could really relate to. Too bad Zack and he were such good friends. . . .

An hour later, he found himself discussing his present life with her and having a great time. But that wasn't what he had come for, and he felt a little tug of guilt every now and then at the way the conversation had turned the tables on him. He should be the one doing the questioning. But she was such a good listener.

"Would you like to discuss Millie?" Toni asked pleasantly as she tried to stifle a bored yawn, referring to his most recent tragic relationship with a woman who worked in a local massage parlor. "I know how unpleasant breaking up with someone you really care for can be."

"No, I don't think so," he replied guiltily, finally realizing he was going to have to turn the conversation around to her. "I'd like to talk about you now, if you don't mind."

"Me?" She laughed. "I'm afraid my life hasn't been nearly as exciting as yours."

"Oh, I wouldn't say that. Zack told me you just came out of a bad relationship yourself," he said encouragingly, hoping she would open up.

"He did?" For a moment she was annoyed. Why

in the world would Zack be telling Jim about her personal life? He knew she didn't like to discuss her recent breakup with just anyone. But as long as he had already told Jim about Skip, she supposed it wouldn't hurt to answer his question. "Yes, as a matter of fact, I did."

"Mmmm." Jim picked up the basket of rolls and extended it to her. "Was it pretty rough on you?"

She shrugged and accepted a piece of the hot bread. "I suppose so."

"Do you talk to yourself out loud sometimes, Toni?" he shot back unexpectedly.

Now, it was odd that he should ask that. "Yes, sometimes."

"Why?" he volleyed back so quickly, it made her nearly drop the roll she had taken.

She quickly recovered the bread and took a bite, chewing thoughtfully for a moment while she pondered his strange question. "Well, it's just sort of a bad habit I've gotten myself into, Jim. How—how did you know I did that?"

"I didn't. I was just making conversation." He smiled politely as he lavishly buttered his roll.

Sheesh! This guy was even stranger than Zack thought *she* was!

"Do you ever talk to yourself?" she turned the tables on him again.

He looked rather uneasy as he picked up his water glass and took a sip out of it. "Occasionally. I suppose everyone does at one time or another."

"Do you ever answer yourself?" she asked teasingly.

"Never."

"Good, that's when they say you're in big trouble."

Reaching for the salt and pepper, Jim sprinkled his salad as he inquired casually, "Zack tells me you saw a flying saucer in his backyard."

This time his question took her by complete surprise. She had thought Zack preferred to keep those little incidents quiet, since he had all but threatened her bodily harm if she didn't keep still about what she had seen. But here he was running around telling all his friends about it.

He was turning out to be a big rat with an even bigger mouth.

She scooted to the edge of her chair and glanced around uneasily. Well, all right. If Jim was asking her if she had actually seen a flying saucer, then she was going to tell him. "Did Zack tell you about the saucer?" she asked in a hushed whisper.

"Yes. Would you like to tell me more about it?"

Her eyes darted around the room frantically, not by choice but because it suddenly felt like one of the lenses had slipped.

With the edge of her fingertip, she made sure the offending object was still in place before she continued. "Well, there isn't much to tell. Actually, I've seen the saucer twice."

"Really?" Jim lifted his brows in interest. "Recently?"

"No, not recently," she had to admit. "The sightings were about two weeks apart."

"Hmmm, how interesting. Did you see these objects in different locations each time?"

"No, both times they were in Zack's backyard," she confessed. "And I only saw two."

"Two, huh? Were you under any particular strain at the time? I mean, other than the one you've been experiencing since your breakup with—with—"

"Skip Harden."

"Yes, Skip. Were these sightings directly after your breakup with Skip?" he inquired pleasantly as he reached for another roll.

She glanced at him warily. Why in the world was he being so nosy? "No, it was a few weeks later," she answered hesitantly. "Why?"

"Oh, no particular reason. Were the saucers doing any thing in particular?" he pursued.

"No, just the normal hovering and glowing that saucers reportedly do." Warming to the subject, she edged closer to him and whispered in an excited voice, "They were big, though. Big with a lot of lights and funny-looking legs for landing gear."

"Really?"

"Yes, really." She couldn't decide if he was really interested in what she had seen or was merely trying to determine if she was just another fruitcake who had only imagined she had witnessed a visit from outer space. "The speed at which they travel, why, you would hardly believe anything could go that fast. One minute I was standing there looking at it, and the next minute it was gone. Poof! Just like that. Up and gone. You wouldn't have believed it unless you were there." She paused again and eyed him suspiciously.

He was looking at her awfully strangely now, almost as if he were studying each word she said. "You *do* believe in flying saucers, don't you?"

"I certainly think the subject is open for discussion," he replied easily.

"Oh. Well, good. Zack doesn't."

"Oh?"

"No, he thinks I'm seeing things."

"Why would he think that?"

"I don't know." She bit into a forkful of her salad thoughtfully. "I think he thinks I'm some sort of screwball."

"And what do you think?"

She put another forkful of salad into her mouth. "I think I saw a flying saucer."

"No, I mean, why would Zack think you're under some sort of strain?" he persisted.

Once more she glanced at him skeptically. "What makes you think Zack thinks I'm under a strain?"

"Oh, he just happened to mention he thought you might be more upset by your breakup with Skip than you think. You know, it goes back to what we were discussing earlier."

My, my. He and Zack *must* have had a long conversation about her. What were the two of them up to?

She placed her fork by her plate carefully. "Well, I appreciate Zackery's concern, but I'm really doing fine, thank you, so you can tell him he can rest assured that I'm not having an emotional breakdown or anything like that, if that's what he's worried about." She looked at him pointedly. "And you can also relay the message that I *did* see the saucer in his backyard whether he cares to believe me or not."

141

"Oh, yeah. If the subject happens to come up, I'll tell him," Jim said, trying to keep his voice deliberately casual. Boy, if she ever found out what he was doing, he and Zack would both be in big trouble. "So you have been under an emotional strain—you admit that."

She bit the corners of her mouth and turned her gaze impatiently toward the ceiling. Apparently Jim was playing amateur psychologist for his friend, and she was getting a little tired of it. "Yes, I have. But I haven't gone off the deep end, if that's what you mean."

"No, no, I didn't mean that at all."

It certainly sounded to her as if that's what he meant.

"Tell me, Toni, why do you think the saucer appeared twice in Zack's backyard?"

She picked up another hot roll and buttered it irritably. "Because it wants his barbecue grill."

"His grill!"

"That's what I think." That ought to blow his mind, she thought gleefully as she bit into the roll and chewed it smugly. "Crazy, isn't it? But that's what I think it wants."

"What makes you think it wants his grill?" Jim asked incredulously.

She looked at him innocently. "Because that's the only thing it seemed interested in. The last ship, which was much larger than the first one, had this funny-looking telescope that had this strange little eye on it. The scope shot out the bottom of the craft and ran over every square inch of Zack's grill. I think it was computing data back to the mother

142

ship, but then I really can't be sure of that. What sort of desserts do they have here?"

He blinked in disbelief. "Uh, gee, I don't know." He absently signaled for the waiter to bring a dessert menu. "A telescope, you say?"

"Yeah. That's what it looked like to me."

"Did you call the authorities?"

"I checked around with a couple of local television stations and called the newspaper and the police department. No one had received any reports of a sighting."

"You didn't report what you had seen?"

"No, at first I wasn't sure myself if that's what it had been. It was the first night I arrived in town, you remember? When you and Zack moved my refrigerator and sofa into the house for me? Well, I was awfully tired from my trip, and I thought perhaps that maybe I didn't see anything after all."

"What made you decide that you had actually seen it?"

"When it came back the second time."

"And you don't find it strange that you're the only one who saw this, uh—unusual occurrence?"

"I'm not the only one who's seen a flying saucer," she denied. "You wouldn't believe the people who've seen them and can't get anyone to believe their stories."

"Why, Dr. Howerton! How nice to see you!" An older couple paused beside their table as Jim nearly choked on a piece of beef that he had just put in his mouth.

He shot a worried glance in Toni's direction and

immediately rose to his feet and shook hands with the gentleman.

"How are you, Frank?"

"Much better, thank you, doctor."

"Toni, I'd like for you to meet Frank and Meredith O'Reilly."

Toni smiled at the newcomers pleasantly. "Hello."

She watched with growing interest as the couple exchanged a few minutes of small talk with Jim before they walked on to their table. Then her face turned sullen as a tiny light popped on in her head. A *doctor!* For Zachery's sake, she sure hoped that his friend was a veterinarian.

"Doctor?" She looked up at Jim as he reseated himself and tried to avoid her accusing gaze. It was all becoming quite clear to her what Zack was up to, and she didn't care for it one little bit.

"Uh, yes. Didn't I mention it? How careless of me. Now, let's see. You asked about dessert." He tried to change the subject as fast as he could.

She quietly put her napkin back on the table.

Why that low-down, conniving *ingrate,* she seethed. He had sicced a psychiatrist on her!

"You're a doctor," she said sweetly. "How interesting. Zack never mentioned that to me."

He shrugged guiltily. "Well, you know Zack. He doesn't say a whole lot."

"No, that little devil, he doesn't, does he? Tell me, Jim, what kind of a doctor are you?"

As if she had to ask. She would bet her last dime that he was a psychiatrist, but she was going to make him squirm before she dragged it out of him.

"Uh, how about the crepes suzettes? They say they're really delicious," he hedged, trying to figure a way out of this sticky situation.

"Crepes. They're nice, but I've suddenly lost my appetite. What kind of a doctor did you say you are, Jim?"

"They have apple pie, too," he suggested weakly. Oh, brother. She had caught on.

"What *kind,* Jim?" Her eyes were still red and weepy, but they had bolts of fire shooting out of them now.

"A psychiatrist," he barely mumbled.

"I should have guessed!" She angrily slapped her hands down on the table and shot to her feet. The force of her blow rattled the dishes and coffee cups on the table, and the diners' heads all whirled around abruptly to see what was going on. "Of all the nerve! You should be ashamed of yourself, Jim Howerton! And so should your friend! Two grown men acting like juvenile delinquents. I'm ashamed of both of you!"

Never one to accept blame when he could avoid it, he quickly defended himself. "It wasn't my idea! It was Zack's!"

"Isn't this just a little unethical for a man in your profession?" she demanded.

"A little." He spoke so low, she could barely hear him. "Sit down, Toni, and I'll explain."

"I don't think you have to explain. I think I know exactly what's going on here, and I don't appreciate it in the least!"

"Zack was only concerned about you—"

"Well, you tell Mr. Tremayne, I'll thank him to stay out of my business!" she nearly shouted.

"Shhh!" He tried helplessly to quiet her, thinking about two of his patients dining at a table close by. What would they think? "He was worried about you."

"Stick it in your ear, Dr. Howerton. There is nothing wrong with me!"

"I know—I know. Shhh." He glanced at the O'Reillys and grinned lamely.

She was so mad, all she could think about was revenge. The very nerve of these two men trying to imply that she was ready to be committed! Well, she may not be able to do anything about one of them at the moment, but she sure could embarrass the pants off the other one!

"You think I'm nuts? Well, I certainly don't want to disappoint you. Watch this, and relay it on to your friend!"

Before Jim could stop her, she whirled around and stuck her thumbs in her ears, screwed up her face, and wiggled her hands frantically in the direction of the O'Reillys. "Yoo-hoo! Frankie and Meredith? I'm nuts, and Jimmy's helping me!" she yelled at the top of her lungs. "I'm seeing flying saucers and little green men, and I'm talking to myself, and—"

Jim lunged for her and smiled weakly at the other diners. "She's a little upset," he apologized as he began to hurriedly drag her out of the room.

Toni knew what she was doing was childish and immature, but it was also just what he deserved.

She was only sorry that the Honorable Judge

Zachery Elsworth Tremayne couldn't be here to get his dose of the medicine, too!

Jim continued to drag her away from the table as the remaining diners gaped in disbelief. Never, as long as he lived, Jim fumed as he hauled her past the frowning headwaiter, would he ever do another friend a favor!

The following morning, Zack was sitting in his chambers going over some papers when the door to his office flew open.

He had been expecting—and dreading—this little visit. Jim had called the night before and had let him know what had happened at the restaurant. He still couldn't believe she had made such a scene!

"Toni! I thought you might drop by—"

Before he could finish the sentence, she marched to his desk and dumped his half-filled coffee cup onto the floor, along with a container of pencils and all the papers that had been on his desk.

Then, picking up the small vase of fresh flowers that remained, she poured it over his head.

Reaching into his back pocket for a clean handkerchief, he calmly mopped at the stream of water dripping in rivulets down his face. "I know you would rather die than let me know it, but you're upset about something, aren't you?"

"You know perfectly well what I'm upset about, you dirty rat!"

"Now, hold on a minute. Jim called me last night and told me what happened, and I want to apologize to you—"

"Save your breath. I don't appreciate you implying to your friends that I'm a loony-tune, Mr. Tremayne. So just stop it!"

"I was only trying to help—"

"Don't even talk to me. Not *ever* again!" She whirled around and headed for the door, then stopped to turn back around and point an accusing finger in his direction. "And not only do I hope that saucer comes back and steals your barbecue grill, but I hope it snatches the pants right off you in the process, you—you—ratfink!"

She went out the door, then slammed it with a resounding bang.

Sighing, Zack reached up and gingerly pulled a daisy out of his hair.

Leaning back in his chair, a slow grin spread across his face and he methodically began to pluck the petals off the flower, one by one. "She loves me, she loves me not . . ."

When the last petal was pulled off and it ended on "she loves me not," he experienced a sharp pang of disappointment at the verdict.

He frowned.

Now, why in the world had he been hoping it would turn out the other way?

CHAPTER NINE

Not that it was any of his business, but he would sure like to know *who* in the hell she had staying over there with her!

Zack was pacing the floor in his living room a few days later and shooting occasional sulking glances out the window.

That just goes to prove that you never really know a person, he grumbled under his breath. His pacing increased in tempo. He would never have believed that Toni Cameron would bring some stray man home, one whom he was sure she barely knew, to stay with her.

But there it was, plain as day.

Some guy had moved in with her over the weekend, and Zack was at a loss to understand who he was or why he was there with her.

Hadn't she just gotten herself out of a mess like that?

If she were still speaking to him, he'd go over there and ask her outright what was going on, but she wasn't. She was still ticked off about Jim, and she had made a point of coldly ignoring him for the past few days.

His gaze resentfully surveyed the man again.

It was a puzzle to him where he came from. As far as he knew, she hadn't even been dating anyone. At least, he hadn't seen anyone coming in and out of her place.

Well, if she were that loose, he had been right not to get involved with her. He shook his head disgustedly. He had thought she was vulnerable, that she wasn't ready for another relationship so soon after breaking up with that Harden guy, and he hadn't wanted to push her.

And he wasn't all that sure he even *wanted* a relationship with her.

Maybe he didn't. He stuck his hands back into his pockets smugly. Then his face fell as he thought about how much he had missed talking to her this week. Maybe he did. . . .

With a sinking feeling in the pit of his stomach, he suddenly realized that that was exactly what he wanted from her.

Sure, there had been other women in his life, but Toni had been different from the very beginning. For the life of him, he couldn't put his finger on the reason why she was different, but she was.

His brow furrowed into another worried frown. Exactly what did he feel for this childlike woman? Protectiveness and friendship—or did it go deeper than that? No, not love—surely not.

The frown deepened to a downright sulk as he slumped down on the sofa and crossed his arms behind his head. He stared up at the ceiling morosely.

Please, Lord, not love. The woman had undoubtedly gone off the deep end. What was he supposed to do with a raving idiot who saw flying saucers in his backyard?

No, he decided firmly, it was only a brother-sister-type feeling he had for her. He loved her and wanted to protect her—he grimaced painfully as he realized that he had used the word *love* again.

No, he argued, Toni Cameron was nothing to him but a friend. Now that she had pulled this little trick of bringing a total stranger home with her, he was going to wash his hands of being her protector once and for all. She was nothing to him, he repeated again, out loud so the statement would have more credibility.

Good Lord. She even had him talking to himself now!

He rose and went back to the window and carefully lifted the corner of the curtain. His eyes ran critically over the man who was busy washing a red Porsche in the drive next door.

At least he had good taste in cars. And he supposed some women would be turned on by his physical type. But he personally found him disgusting.

He had had plenty of time to reach his conclusion. He had watched the man like a hawk ever since his arrival Friday night.

The precision-cut, rust-colored hair was carefully blown dry and sprayed. The expensive sport shirt and tennis shorts he was wearing were designed to show off the fact that he was a health club nut. His biceps flexed proudly in the hot afternoon sun as the man energetically scrubbed at the car, and the muscles of his sturdy, sun-bronzed legs were stretched taut. No doubt this man was a pretty impressive sight to *her,* but to Zack he looked a little questionable.

A pretty boy was what he appeared to be to Zack —that is, if he had to pick a nice word to describe him.

Letting the curtain drop back into place, Zack ambled over to his desk and tried to divert his mind from what was going on next door.

Personally, he didn't care what was going on.

But she sure had fooled him.

An hour later, he gave up all pretense of being indifferent and fixed himself a glass of iced tea. He had no idea how it had happened, but whether he liked it or not, his feelings for Toni Cameron had grown far beyond being friendly neighbors, and he might as well face it.

Picking up the glass, he went out to the backyard to try to get his mind off his troubles.

He slumped down in a chaise longue and took a sip of his tea, staring glumly at the spot his barbecue grill used to inhabit.

Where in the devil had it disappeared to?

The sound of Toni's voice echoed loudly in his ear. "The saucer took it . . . the saucer took it . . . the saucer took it."

He groaned out loud.

Ever since she had moved to town, things had just not gone well for him at all.

As if she hadn't already had more than her share of bad luck, Skip had to show up on her front doorstep.

Toni was out hoeing in her small garden, trying to

152

work off some nervous energy and get her mind off her problems. You could have knocked her over with a feather when she had opened the door late Friday evening and seen her old boyfriend standing there.

She reached up to wipe the perspiration from her brow as she remembered that unnerving incident.

"Hi, doll," he had said, just as if nothing at all had changed between them.

"Skip! What in the world are you doing here?" She was sure she looked every bit as stunned as she felt. What *was* he doing here?

"Is that any way to greet an old friend?" He stepped inside the door, and before she could prevent it, he had scooped her up in his arms and was kissing her in an exuberant hello.

A thrill of excitement shot through her as his familiar scent and touch enveloped her. No matter what their problems, they had always been highly attracted to each other, and she guessed she hadn't succeeded in getting over that physical feeling for him as easily as she had gotten over the emotions.

She hated herself, but she found herself kissing him back, forgetting for the time being that this was Skip, the man who had caused her nothing but trouble.

"Now, that's my dollface," he chuckled wickedly as their mouths finally parted long minutes later. He rubbed his nose against hers. "I knew you'd be glad to see me."

He was the same old Skip, she thought resentfully. Cocksure and needing to be taken down about five notches. Well, she had her whittling knife all ready.

Backing away from him before he tried to kiss her again, she closed the door and walked a safe distance across the floor before she turned to face him. "How did you find me?"

"I have connections." He glanced around the small apartment nonchalantly. "Nice. But it's a little small, isn't it?"

"Not for me. I like it."

"Well"—he grinned and took a few cautious steps closer to her—"that's all that counts." When he was within reaching distance, his arm snaked out with lightning speed and captured her once more. He kissed her again, but this time she managed to break it off and move away from him before she found herself responding.

Noting her coolness, he shrugged and dropped his arms reluctantly to his side. "Hey, the apartment's nice, and I suppose we can get by on a little less room," he murmured cajolingly.

She shot him a withering look. "What are you doing here, Skip?" she demanded again.

He smiled at her patiently. "A little of this, a little of that."

"What's that supposed to mean?" He had always had an infuriating way of beating around the bush.

"Oh, I thought I'd come down here and look things over and see you. Find out how you're doing."

"I'm doing fine. And I intend to keep it that way," she said with a distinct note of warning in her voice.

The million-dollar smile that had been so winning a few moments before dulled somewhat as he realized that his charms were not affecting her the way they usually did. "You're still mad, and I don't blame you. I acted pretty rotten, but I was hoping you were ready to let bygones be bygones." He sighed. "I've missed you, doll."

"Well, you can forget about letting bygones be bygones. Yes, you were rotten, and yes, I'm still mad, and think again if you think we can make due with less room." She had not failed to notice his earlier reference concerning the apartment. "I don't know what you're up to, Skip, but count me out of your plans." Her tone immediately softened as she saw hurt cross his face. "Look, I'm sorry. Okay? I don't want to hurt you, but what we had is over, Skip, and I don't ever want to get in a situation like that again."

Once again the smile brightened as he threw his hands up in complete innocence. "Hey, baby, I'm not trying to push in on you. I just thought you might put me up for a few days while I look around. I know you need a little more time to get your priorities straightened out."

"I'm not the local Howard Johnson's, Skip, and I've had two years to think about my priorities," she snapped. "Can't you rent a motel room like anyone else?"

"Well, I'm a little short of funds at the moment," he confessed. "You know, ever since we broke up, I've had a lot of financial problems."

She laughed ironically. "Life hasn't exactly been

a bed of roses for me, either. What happened to your part of the savings?"

Even with Skip's tendency to overspend, she had managed to save quite a nice little nest egg for the two of them while they had been together.

"Oh, that." She took heart as she saw that he at least had the decency to look shamefaced while confessing what he had done with his part of the money. "I was so torn up after you left that I went completely crazy. In an effort to get my mind off you, I went out and bought that Porsche I had been talking about." He shrugged sheepishly. "I'm afraid I spent every penny."

That didn't surprise her a bit. He had wanted a Porsche ever since she had met him, and somehow, someway, he had always managed to get what he wanted.

But it still irritated her that he was managing to make it sound as if it were all her fault that he was broke.

"I hope that useless squandering helped salve your conscience," she returned coolly.

"No, it didn't, baby. I've been miserable without you," he confessed.

She was totally unimpressed by the whipped-dog act he had decided to hand her now. Skip Harden should have been an actor. He would have surely won an Academy Award for this performance.

"So you spent all your money. You still have your business, don't you?"

"I sold it. The buyer took me to the cleaners, but I wanted out." He stepped forward again, and Toni cautiously took another step backward. "Don't be afraid of me, doll." His expression suddenly grew very childlike. "I've missed you, Toni. I'm no good without you. I was hoping you'd missed me, too, and that maybe we could start all over. I'm ready for marriage now," he admitted. "You set the date, and I'll be waiting at the altar to meet you."

It was so uncharacteristic of Skip to make such a statement that she had no choice but to believe that he was sincere in his proposal.

"Thank you for the offer, but I'm afraid it's too late for marriage now," she refused gently.

"Oh, come on, baby."

"Don't start with me," she warned. She knew his sneaky tactics by heart. Soften her up, make her feel sorry for him, and he would soon have her eating out of his hand.

It had always worked well for him in the past, and she had to admit that once or twice she had felt her resolve waver. After all, she had loved him very dearly at one time.

But this time his pleas fell on deaf ears.

"If you spent your money on a car, then that's your fault, not mine. And I have no intention of picking up where we left off. I'm very happy with the way my life is right now. I'm sorry, Skip, but I don't love you anymore."

"Is there another man?" he asked quietly. This wasn't his Toni at all. She had changed, matured.

"No." She thought of Zack and wished she could say there was. "No, I guess I've just fallen out of love. I'm sorry."

She was stubborn when she wanted to be, and Skip knew her every bit as well as she knew him.

"Okay, okay," he returned in a placating tone. "Just let me stay with you until I can check out the job situation here in town."

He could work on changing her mind later on. He was going to need some time to update his tactics for this new woman.

As much as she would have preferred to tell him to get along little dogie, she supposed that he had just as much right to live in this town as she did.

"Just a few days," he pleaded. "I won't get in your way, and when I get back on my feet, I'll pay you back for letting me stay here."

"You bet you will," she agreed firmly. His line of credit was now defunct with her. "With interest."

Her attention was diverted back to her work when a rabbit scurried past her feet and darted through the pole beans.

"Get!" She shooed the pesky animal off with the tip of her hoe and went back to work. She had to suppress a smile when she thought of how Zack had been peeking out his window all weekend. He was a fool if he thought she hadn't seen him gawking behind the curtain like one of those nosy neighbors he was always talking about. He had to be wondering who was staying with her, but she'd be darned if she was going to call and let him know it was Skip. He would start in on her about going back to her former lover, and that was the last thing she needed right now—especially since she had come to the sickening conclusion that she had fallen in love with her neighbor.

She stopped again and pushed her damp hair up

off her forehead. It was too hot to be hoeing, but she had to work off her frustrations.

A few moments later the top of a man's head popped up on the other side of the fence, then quickly disappeared again.

Toni had caught the movement out of the corner of her eye, but she decided to ignore it.

It was probably him spying on her again, and she was still not speaking to the traitor.

She supposed that he was hoping to catch her foaming at the mouth or something.

The dark blond head bobbed up and down again twice more in quick succession before she decided to call a halt to his less-than-discreet surveillance.

"Do you want something in particular, Zackery?" she demanded, leaning on her hoe and eyeing the fence with hostility.

It took a moment, but he soon realized that he was trapped. Slowly his face reemerged over the boards, wearing a sheepish grin. "Hi there."

"Hi there," she returned, none too nicely. It was hot and miserable, and she was in no mood to confront him. She turned her back on him and went back to weeding the garden.

"Hot out here today, isn't it?" He propped his arms on the fence and peeked over at her hopefully.

She grunted and kept on working.

"You still mad at me?" Funny how she seemed to grow prettier every day. His eyes lingered hungrily on her shapely outline.

"Yes, I am."

"I thought so."

There was a few moments of silence while she worked and he thought.

"Who's the guy?"

"None of your business." She wasn't about to ease the curiosity that apparently was about to kill him.

He gazed up in the sky and vowed to keep his patience with her. "You seen anything of my barbecue grill?"

Her hoe paused, and she glanced up at him irritably. "No, why? Is it gone?"

"Yeah. I figure some neighborhood kid took it."

Her mouth dropped open at this unexpected news, and a thrill of elation shot through her. So the saucer *did* come back and get the grill! But she'd be willing to bet her last dime that he wouldn't believe her, and she certainly wasn't in any mood to try and convince him again, so she merely dropped her eyes back to the ground again and viciously uprooted a clump of weeds. "Hah."

"What's that supposed to mean?"

"It means, hah! I could tell you in a minute where your barbecue grill went, but you would only accuse me of being crazy—again!" she added in a snappish afterthought.

He sighed tolerantly. "No, I wouldn't. Whether you want to believe it or not, I don't think you're crazy. I'm concerned about you. That's all."

She kept her eyes on her work and tried to ignore him.

"Okay. Where do you think my barbecue grill is?" he asked a few moments later, knowing exactly what she was going to say.

160

She leaned on her hoe and jabbed her finger upward in exasperation. "Guess!"

He grinned. "Those thievin' little monsters. Do you suppose they're having a party up there and forgot to ask us?"

"Very funny."

In an effort to appease her, he wiggled his brows at her affectionately. "I'd take you, if the little green devils would ask us."

"I'd sooner go out with a goat," she informed him.

He chuckled, then watched her in silence for a few moments. "So you really think it was the flying saucer that came back and snatched my grill?"

"It's gone, isn't it?"

"Yes."

"I assume you've reported it to the police, and they have been unable to locate it?"

"Yeah."

"*You* haven't been able to find it anywhere?"

"No."

"I saw a flying saucer looking it over very carefully." She narrowed her eyes, daring him to dispute her next words. "Didn't I?"

He grinned and shrugged his shoulders agreeably; he wanted to get back in her good graces. "So you say."

"I rest my case."

He sighed again. She might have a point. Stranger things had been known to happen, and the darn thing had disappeared awfully suddenly.

"All right. In the name of peace, let's say I accept that theory for the time being. I'm tired of this cold war, and I'm sorry I made you mad," he apologized. "But I had nothing but the best intentions when I asked Jim to talk to you." He leaned over the fence and put a restraining hand on her hoe as his eyes pleaded silently with hers for forgiveness. "Let's kiss and make up."

There was something about Zack Tremayne that made it terribly hard for her to stay mad at him—or else she was just a born sucker. Her hoe paused in midair as she took his apology into consideration.

She might accept it, but she had to know one thing first.

"What did Jim say about my state of mental health?" she asked hesitantly.

"He told me you are mean as the devil, *never* to take you to Poochie's again, and that you are without a doubt as sane as I am."

She glanced up and grinned impishly. "And that's supposed to make me feel better?"

"It should."

"And Jim doesn't think I'm crazy?"

"No, not at all." Zack paused, debating whether to tell her everything Jim had said. The words would be hard to say, but he loved her enough—yes, loved.

It was painfully clear to him now. He was crazy in love with her. He had stopped fighting that fact the moment he had seen her again today. But he loved her enough to want her happiness at any cost, and if that meant her going back to that bum she had been living with, well, he would just have to face it. "He said he felt you had been under a strain, as anyone would be after a breakup with someone

162

they loved, and he thought that you might want to consider going back to Skip and trying to work out your differences, if that would make you happy. These things have a way of working themselves out if two people love each other."

She knew it! He was back to that again.

"Well, tell Jim I appreciate his advice, and you two can stop worrying about me. I'll be fine," she said coolly, then turned her attention back to her work.

She could have told him she wasn't going back to Skip, that that was the last thing on earth that would make her happy, but she declined. It hurt to think that he was so blind, he couldn't see it was him that she wanted, not Skip Harden.

Reaching out to tweak her nose, he smiled at her tenderly. "I'm trying to quit worrying, but you've become very special to me, Toni."

"You've become special to me, too, Zack."

"Then is my humble apology accepted, or do I have to get down on the ground and eat dirt to get back in your good graces?"

His touch made her weak with longing, and she felt her anger melting away. "That might be fun to watch, but you don't have to go to those lengths. Apology accepted."

She held out her hand in friendship, but instead of shaking it as she expected, he pulled her up to the fence and proceeded to kiss her—lightly at first, then with hunger that stunned her.

If he thought she would protest, he was in for the shock of his life. On the contrary, her arms went

163

around his neck, and they kissed deeply for a few minutes.

"I think I'd like to discuss this further," he murmured between snatches of heated kisses. Seconds later, he had jumped the fence, and when he took her in his arms, they kissed until she was fairly breathless.

"I've missed you, funnyface," he murmured with a low groan. "Really missed you."

She closed her eyes and savored the feel of him pressed tightly against her.

"Now, before I go nuts, will you please tell me who this guy is?" he pleaded in a husky voice. His hands caressed the sides of her bare arms, and then he brought her back into another nearly bone-crunching embrace. It was as if he wanted to pull her inside of him and make them one.

"It's Skip," she confessed.

For some reason, that was not what he had expected to hear. At the mention of her former boyfriend's name, Zack's face clouded with anger.

"Skip? The Skip—the guy you used to live with?"

"Yeah, that's the only Skip I know," she confirmed hesitantly, sensing his sudden change of attitude.

"What's he doing at your house?" Zack suddenly backed away from her, a cold, sickening stab of jealousy slicing through his middle.

"He's just here to visit for a few days," she explained.

"Visit?"

"Yes. He's looking for a job."

"He's going to *live* here?" The jealousy was now

an acute, agonizing pain in the middle of his stomach. Granted, he had been encouraging her to try to reconcile with Skip—but if she actually should, he didn't know if he could take it or not, no matter what he had previously thought.

"Yeah, I think so." She was confused by the look on Zack's face. He looked upset, almost sick, and yet she had thought he would be elated to hear that Skip was back.

"And he's staying with you?" he asked, a certain coolness invading his tone.

"Yes," she said honestly, "but—"

"How cozy." Zack's arms dropped to his side limply. "I'm sure that makes you feel better."

"It doesn't mean anything," Toni found herself defending quickly. She didn't want him to get the wrong impression.

The thought of Toni in some other man's arms sleeping right next door to him made him literally sick to his stomach. "Yeah, I'm sure. Well, hey. I have to go."

"Zack." Before she knew what she was doing, she had reached out and drawn him back to her, savoring the feel of him for one more moment. She knew Zack Tremayne would never view her as anything but a good friend, but that didn't keep her from loving him. "I'm honestly not mad at you anymore," she consoled. "And I do appreciate your concern."

He knew she was another man's woman, but at that moment she was his Toni, and her soft, pink lips were too much of a temptation for him. His

165

arms came back around her slender waist, and their mouths met again . . . and again . . . and again.

When he finally set her aside, they both ached with desire and a deep sense of hopelessness.

"I'll be seeing you," Zack murmured.

"Yeah."

They kissed once more, lingeringly, then he was back over the fence and out of sight, leaving Toni choking back the gathering tears.

The saucer might have stolen his grill, but he had gotten what he deserved, she sniffed, leaning forlornly on her hoe.

Because Zackery Tremayne had stolen her heart, and that was much more valuable than any darned old grill.

CHAPTER TEN

"Yes, Mother. I know he's a louse and will never amount to anything." Toni sighed and shifted around uncomfortably in her seat.

Unfortunately, Skip had answered the phone this afternoon while Toni was at work, and it had been her mother calling.

Needless to say, the phone had been ringing off the hook when she'd arrived home that evening.

"No, Mother. It isn't all starting up again. I told you. He's merely staying here while he looks for a job."

She tapped her hands impatiently on the table and rolled her eyes upward. "Because he didn't have anywhere else to stay. Believe me, I don't want him here any more than you do."

She got up and poked the tip of her finger into the wilted philodendron plant on the windowsill, then dumped a glass of water onto it. "As soon as he's found a job. . . . I don't know. He's looking every day, that's all I know."

Her eyes wandered wistfully over to Zack's backyard, where he was just hauling a trash bag out the back door.

It had been almost a week since he had talked to her at the fence, and the memory of his kisses still sent white heat searing through her.

Zack glanced over in her direction, a habit that was painfully familiar to her, and she leaned over and pecked on the window to gain his attention.

"I'm just pecking on the window, Mother."

Zack grinned and winked at her, and her pulse raced feverishly. He looked absolutely delectable in an old pair of faded jeans and ragged sweat shirt, and she longed to run out and throw herself in his arms.

"Just my neighbor. He's taking his trash out."

She grinned back at Zack and waved.

He returned the wave, then disappeared around the side of his house, dragging the trash bag behind him.

"No, Mother. There isn't anything funny going on between me and him," she said irritably, and turned her attention back to the wilted plant. "Good grief, I don't hop into bed with every man I meet."

Not that she wouldn't have given it some serious thought in Zackery's case, but—

"Well, I'm sorry, but I don't think that was very nice of you to say that, either."

She sighed again. "I don't know. Thirty-seven or thirty-eight. . . . Very nice looking. . . . No, he isn't married. . . . I don't know. I see a few women going in and out over there. I'm sure he's a perfectly healthy male and has all the female companionship he wants."

Brother, was that an understatement! But if she

had told her mother how many women actually went in and out of Zack's on a weekly basis, her mother would be on the next bus to save her daughter from the evil clutches of the dirty old man next door.

But he seemed to be changing. She had not noticed one single woman around his doorstep this past week.

"Mother! How should I know if he's a Methodist? I don't keep track of his religious preferences. I just live next to the man. . . . Okay. If he happens to ask me to marry him while he's taking his trash out some morning, I'll make sure he's not a heathen. Does that relieve your mind?"

Toni loved her mother as much as anyone loved a parent, but there were times . . .

"Oh, look, don't be upset. I'm sorry, okay? I'm just a little testy lately, and I say things I shouldn't," she apologized, and plopped back into the chair.

She had been more than testy. This week had been miserable, with Skip hanging around and Zack keeping his distance. She really didn't know how much more she was going to be able to take.

"Yes, I'm eating right. . . . I feel fine, really. . . . Well, I can't help it if I sound like I'm not feeling fine. I am—you'll just have to take my word for it. . . . At least eight hours every night."

She groaned silently. "Yes, I eat lots of fruit and whole wheat bread to keep me regular. How's Dad? . . . He shouldn't be doing that. The doctor told him to take it easy. . . . Okay. I'll talk to you in a few days. . . . No, I promise. I'll call. . . . Okay, if I don't, you can call me. . . . Do you want me to take an oath in blood? I swear on Grandmother Plachie's grave, I won't drop off the face of the earth. I'll call you next week, Mom. . . . Okay. I love you. . . . Give Dad my love and tell him not to overdo it. . . . Yes, one day next week. I promise. . . . Okay. 'Bye."

Toni hung up the receiver and threw her head back in the chair to stare morosely up at the ceiling.

The things a daughter had to do to keep peace!

If Toni's week had been bad, Zack's had been even worse.

He had a crick in his neck from straining behind the curtain to keep a close watch of what went on next door, and his jealousy gnawed away at him every day.

The bum was still over there, so undoubtably they had reconciled. The mere thought of that man holding Toni in his arms and making love to her made his blood run cold.

He should be the one doing that, not Skip Harden.

Friday morning, he stepped out of the shower and toweled himself dry irritably. Another sleepless night had passed, and he felt tired and grouchy and out of sorts with the whole world.

Squirting a gob of shaving cream into his hand, he slapped it onto his face carelessly and stared back at his reflection in the mirror.

If he were any man at all, he would go over there and give that Harden a run for his money. After all,

170

Toni might be living with him again, but she wasn't married to him.

He frowned as he brought the razor up to his face. At least, he hoped she wasn't.

Surely he hadn't rushed her off to the altar. Zack had watched her house diligently, and there had been no sign of anything like that happening.

Toni had gone to work every morning and come back home at about the same time every night.

In fact, he hadn't seen her go out at all in the evening since Harden had arrived.

He let out a low curse as he nicked himself. Why couldn't the man leave well enough alone? he fumed and reached for the styptic stick. Given time, Toni would have gotten over him completely. Zack would have personally seen to that.

As he dressed, his irritability grew. Why was he sitting over here mooning over her like a sick calf? Why wasn't he in there vying for her attention just as Harden was?

He was just as capable of marrying her as Skip was. . . .

His hand paused as he angrily jerked a tight knot in his tie. Funny, here he was seriously thinking about marriage to a woman he had only officially been out with one time in his life. But living right next door to her, he felt he knew her habits and her one-of-a-kind personality about as well as anyone. Besides, even though he officially hadn't dated her, he had spent a lot of time with her, had had many long talks . . . exchanged many a long kiss.

A wry chuckle escaped him as he thought about

171

the words he had just used in describing Toni Cameron.

One of a kind. Well, that she was, but that's why he loved her.

And was there anything seriously wrong with her state of mind? He stared into the mirror pensively. No, not really. She had just been a little unsettled for a while after the breakup, but now that Skip was back in her life, she seemed to be fine.

He had no idea what it was that she had seen in his backyard, but other than those incidents and the little odd quirks almost everyone had, she seemed to be sound.

After all, the human race was a pretty strange breed, when you got right down to it, and everyone had a few little idiosyncrasies that could be misinterpreted as loony if the person were caught unawares.

His eyes automatically sought to catch a brief glance of her as he walked to his car ten minutes later.

She wasn't standing in the window as she usually was, and he felt a sharp stab of disappointment before he realized that she probably wasn't even up yet. Because of an early-morning meeting in his chambers, he was leaving much earlier today than he usually did.

It was the beginning of a beautiful day, he noted with little enthusiasm as he turned the key in the ignition. The sun was just breaking over the crest of the old trees behind her house, spreading its warm rays over the earth. The pleasant smell of newly mown grass, kissed by dew, filled the air.

Her bedroom windows faced the east, and he thought how nice it would be to lie in bed with her in his arms on a glorious morning such as this and watch the sun come up together.

In fact, he thought it might be nice to start every day with her in his arms . . . or making love to her while she was still soft and warm and drowsy from sleep. . . .

By the time he pulled his car into his parking place at the courthouse, he was aching with desire for the woman who lived next door. If he didn't think she was happy with Skip back in her life, he would be tempted to go to her this morning and tell her how he felt.

These feelings were new and puzzling, yet oddly exciting. No woman had ever affected him this way before, and yet now he was going to be denied the chance to tell her of his love.

The day dragged on sluggishly. At midmorning, Zack threw his pencil onto his desk and stood up to stretch. He hadn't been able to keep his mind on his work.

He had called his secretary "Toni" twice already, and since her name was Wanda, she had looked at him rather strangely.

He wandered out into the hall toward the coffee machine, and his spirits lifted when he saw Toni emerge from one of the courtrooms.

It was hard to tell whose smile was brighter as they hurried toward each other.

"Hi!"

"Hi." Her eyes eagerly surveyed him standing before her, and her smile widened. "I was worried about you."

"Me? Why?"

"I didn't see you leave for work this morning, and I thought perhaps you might not be feeling well."

"Oh, no. I feel great. I just had an early-morning meeting in my chambers," he explained. "I left about an hour earlier than I usually do."

"Well, that explains it."

"I knew you weren't up when I didn't see you standing at the window the way you usually do."

"No, I probably wasn't. I'm a lazy-head in the mornings."

The pit of Zack's stomach ached as he thought about her lying in bed with Harden, doing—He didn't even want to think about what they might have been doing. "Yeah, I am too. Coffee?"

"Yes, thanks."

"How's Skip?" he asked politely, really not caring how the man was but trying to get a few more minutes with her.

"Fine. How's Karol?"

"Fine."

"I haven't seen her around much lately," Toni prompted, trying to keep her voice light and casual but dying to know what was going on in his life.

"No, we haven't been seeing a whole lot of each other lately." Zack handed her a paper cup. "We've both been busy."

"Yes, I know what you mean."

She was wearing the red dress he was so fond of, and it made the encounter that much more painful as he tried to keep his gaze from being downright lustful.

They stood and drank their coffee, idly chatting for a few more minutes, before Toni glanced at her watch and groaned. "Oh, gee. I'm going to be late." She handed him her half-full cup and picked up the stack of papers she had left on a nearby chair. "I have to rush. See you later."

He stood watching her go down the hallway with a deep ache in his heart.

Glancing down at the cup in his hand, he smiled as he saw the faint traces of her lipstick on the rim.

Raising the cup, he touched his mouth to the outline of her lips, as his eyes, dark with desire, followed her until she disappeared through a large set of wooden doors at the end of the hall.

When Toni walked to her car late that afternoon, she couldn't believe her eyes when she saw Zack leaning against the hood waiting for her.

It wasn't that she wasn't thrilled to see him; her accelerated heart rate told her that that would be a lie. But in a way she almost wished he hadn't been there.

All afternoon she had forced herself to put him out of her mind and concentrate on her work. But it had been hard.

"Hi. What's up?" She paused in front of him and shaded her eyes against the hot late-afternoon sun.

"Nothing. I thought I'd just hang around and see if you had car trouble or anything."

She looked at the car, then back at him. "Why would I have car trouble?"

"I don't know that you will, but I'd hate for you to be stranded here if you did," he theorized. "It's awfully hot out here, and other people have been having problems with their cars."

She shrugged and walked over and opened the car door. It felt like a blast oven inside as she slid behind the wheel and inserted the key into the ignition. "Thanks a lot, but I think I'll be fine. . . ." Her voice trailed off as the starter ground away loudly.

Pumping the foot pedal, she tried again. She grew more puzzled by the minute. Her car had always been dependable, so why all of a sudden didn't it want to start?

"I don't know how you knew I was going to have car trouble," she confessed as the stifling heat forced her back out of the car. "But the darned thing won't start."

"I'll take you home."

"Would you mind?"

He moved away from his casual position on the hood and took hold of her arm, a suspicious grin on his face now. "Not at all."

His car was farther down in the parking area, and they chatted pleasantly as they walked. Toni had a strange feeling that he had deliberately planned this whole thing, but she couldn't figure out why.

If Zack wanted to see her, all he had to do was ask.

"I suppose you have to get straight home," he remarked as he started the car and flipped on the air conditioner to high.

"No, not particularly. Why?"

176

He glanced at her expectantly. "Won't Skip be waiting for you?"

She immediately turned her face away and looked out the window. "No, I don't think so."

"You sure?"

"Positive."

Well, he wasn't about to insist she go home to him. Let Harden fight his own battles. He had offered to take her home.

Zack pulled out of the parking lot and merged into the ongoing traffic. "Want to get a bite to eat before we go home?"

"Sure."

"How about Colonel Sanders?"

"Sounds good."

By the time they had eaten and gotten back into the car, the sun had set. The air was beginning to cool down, and it was a pleasant ride home.

As always, they had laughed and found it very easy to talk with each other. There was something indefinably wonderful about the way she felt when she was with him.

It was a comfortable feeling, yet his nearness always set her senses to tingling.

When they pulled up into Zack's drive, she was still laughing over some silly little incident that had happened that day.

He came around to her side and helped her out of the car, and then they both walked over to the hedge together.

"Well, I guess you'll need to be going in." He paused and put both his hands in his pockets so he wouldn't be tempted to take her in his arms.

"Yes, I guess I'd better. It's been a long day."

"It's still early."

"Yeah, I know. Want to come over and sit in the swing with me awhile?" She peered up at him, and he tried to avoid her gaze. She had beautiful eyes, and he sincerely wished she didn't look so damned kissable all the time.

"No, I guess I'd better not. We wouldn't want to get Skip all upset."

Casting her eyes away guiltily, she sighed. "He—he wouldn't get upset. Come on."

They stepped over the hedge and headed for the side porch. "Why wouldn't he be upset? I sure would be if another man were sitting in the swing with you," Zack blurted out before he knew it.

"You would?" Her eyes snapped back up to meet his.

He was powerless to avoid her gaze this time. "Darn it—yes, I would."

She paused on the second step and tilted her head sideways a fraction. "Why?"

"Why? Well—because. If I were Skip, I would figure you were mine, and if you were mine, I wouldn't want any other man near you."

His words sent shivers of delight through her. To be his—what a marvelous thought. She inserted the key into her door, her mind whirling.

Just exactly what was Zack trying to tell her? That he might be interested in her if Skip weren't in the picture?

Surely not. But if by some small miracle he *was* trying to let her know he was interested . . .

And she wasn't being fair with him by letting him

continue to think that she was Skip's, even though it would probably upset him when he found out she hadn't reconciled with him after all.

Maybe she should clear her conscience and test the water at the same time, just to see what he was getting at.

"But I'm not Skip's," she confessed softly, so softly he almost didn't hear her.

"What?"

"I said, I'm not Skip's," she repeated more firmly.

His face suddenly took on a stormy look. "You mean you're just living with the guy again, but you have no plans of marrying him?"

"No, I'm not living with him, and I'm certainly not going to marry him!" she returned sharply. "So you might as well forget about starting in on me again. I don't love Skip Harden, and I'm not about to go back to him just because you and Jim think that's what I ought to do. It's my life, Zack, and I'm not about to live it with someone I don't love just to make you guys happy!"

Zack could hardly believe her words as he slumped weakly against the doorframe. "You don't love him?"

"No. Not anymore."

"But he's staying here—"

"He *was* staying here. He left yesterday."

"And you let him go?"

"Let him? I insisted he leave."

"I don't understand. What am I supposed to think? The guy you lived with two years suddenly shows back up on your doorstep, and he stays for nine days!"

"I thought that would make you happy. Besides, he was here only eight days!"

"It was nine!"

"Oh, you're counting the Friday night he arrived, and that's not fair!"

"Whatever. He was here too darned long!"

"I agree, but he was trying to find a job."

"Oh, brother. I've heard it all now."

"He was," she defended. "But he couldn't find one, so I told him I didn't care where he went, he couldn't stay here any longer."

"And he accepted that?"

"There wasn't anything else he could do."

"Did he try to get you back into his bed?" Zack's eyes narrowed angrily at the thought.

"Well, yes, but I didn't go."

"Are you sure—"

"Oh, for heavens sake!" She threw the door open angrily and marched into the apartment. "No, I didn't go! How could you think that of me?"

"It was easy," he protested as he followed her into the apartment. "You let me. You even encouraged it," he accused.

The fact that Toni was not Skip Harden's was just beginning to sink in on him, and he was weak with relief.

"I did not, and you're beginning to sound just like my mother. Do you really think that I go to bed with just anyone? For your information, Zachery, I view sex as a very binding arrangement. At the time I lived with Skip, I loved him and was committed to him in every way except by marriage. But let me warn you, the next time I go to bed with a man, it

180

will be because of love *and* commitment—on both sides. Got that?"

"Got it." A slow grin spread across his face as he reached out and pulled her up close to him. "And as long as you brought up the subject, how would you feel about going to bed with me?"

Without blinking an eye she looked at him and said, "I thought you'd never ask."

"You mean, you would?"

"I would if I thought you really loved me—as I love you."

His face broke out in a wide grin. "You love me?"

"I know you think I'm crazy about half the time, and I am—about you," she confessed.

"Oh, Toni." His face instantly turned serious. "I love you—you have to believe that."

With a squeal of joy she flew into his arms, and they kissed until they were both breathless with emotion.

"Oh, Zack," she whispered as their mouths were finally able to break apart for a moment. "This is all so wonderful, finding out you actually love me as much as I love you. I can hardly believe it." She kissed him again to make sure he was really there.

She really didn't know how he felt about the subject of marriage. She wasn't going to repeat her past mistake this time, no matter how much she loved him. "Zachery, how do you feel about marriage?"

"I think marriage is a perfectly acceptable institution."

"If you like living in institutions," she finished the old joke wryly.

"I think I'd like living anywhere with you, Ms.

181

Cameron." His gaze grew incredibly tender as he reached out to touch the tip of her nose. "In fact, I've just been thinking about asking you to marry me. How would you feel about that?"

"I'd feel very good about that," she said softly.

"And do you think you might?"

"It's possible," she teased.

"Well, first"—he scooped her up into his arms— "I think I'd better see what I'm getting myself into."

She frowned at him warningly.

"Hey, look. We're officially engaged now," he protested.

"Yes, but that isn't like being married," she argued, still not at all sure she wasn't being taken in again.

"You're going to have to learn to trust me, funnyface. From this day forward." He knew she had been misled once before in her life, and he wanted her to know that she could always depend on him.

"Can I?"

He leaned forward and touched his nose to hers. "By the time I get through with you, you're going to believe everything I say, lady, for the rest of your life."

She grinned at him. "I assume you know where the bedroom is?"

"Yeah, I spotted that a *long* time ago."

The moonlight made pretty, symmetrical shadows across the bed as Zack carried her into the room.

It was time for love and not for reflection about

182

the past, so Toni put aside all her doubts as he let her slide seductively down the length of his masculine frame. She could feel what her nearness had done to him, and her fingers tightened in his hair as they exchanged a long, welcoming kiss.

The only sounds in the still night were sighs of love as their mouths came together again and as they stood in the middle of the room holding each other.

At first they touched each other gently in a loving exploration of each other; then as their passion grew, so did their eagerness to know one another.

"Did I mention I think you have the best set of legs of any women on earth?" Zack murmured as he began to carefully remove her clothing. The thought of actually being able to feel her next to him without the cumbersome burden of clothing sent his blood racing to a feverish pitch.

"Oh? And just what makes you such an authority on women's legs?" she challenged, then clamped her hand over his mouth for fear he would tell her. "Never mind, I'll accept the compliment."

He chuckled deep in his throat and gently kissed the perfumed softness of her bare skin as he began to unfold her beauty. "You're beautiful, Toni. Not just your legs, but your heart, and that's what makes me love you."

His words were spoken with such sincerity, they brought tears to her eyes. "Thank you, Zackery."

She finally stood before him, vulnerable and naked. His mouth refused to leave hers as he eased out of his own clothes, and then he picked her up and laid her on the bed gently, like a rare and beautiful jewel that had been given to him, his deep, unmistakable love for her radiating from his eyes.

"There will still be a legal ceremony, but I take you, Toni, as my wife, to love, honor, and cherish, for as long as we both shall live," he whispered, and then with agonizing sweetness he began to show her just how right their love was.

Their kisses were searching and feverish as he brought her up to his bare loins. The feel of his body pressing tightly against hers sent a wild surge of joy through her, and she wanted more, much more. But suddenly his mouth jerked away from hers, and he searched deep within her eyes as if a horrible thought had suddenly occurred to him. "I love you, Toni. For me, you are the only woman I have ever said that to. But I have to know—"

"What, darling?" She could see the agony written in his troubled gaze, and she wondered what could have brought it on, especially at this moment.

"Skip," he answered miserably. "I know he's out of your life, but is he out of your heart?"

She laughed and cradled his face in both her hands as she sought to lay his fears to permanent rest. "There isn't even a fraction of an inch left in my heart to harbor love for any man except you, Zackery. Skip was gone long ago, darling. Now and forever, there is only room for you."

"You're sure?"

"I'm very sure. But I could ask you the same of Karol."

"I was never in love with Karol," he stated simply.

"And all the other women?"

"I've told you before, there were not that many other women that I was seeing on a personal basis. The few that I did, well"—he kissed her again suggestively—"we were like ships in the night. I wouldn't have thought about tying any one of them up in my harbor."

"But you would me?"

"I would you."

Her sigh of relief was muffled as he took the initiative once again in their lovemaking, and there was no longer any doubt about where their love lay as he claimed her for his own.

Later, when their passion had been spent, they lay exhausted in each other's arms, holding each other tightly.

Toni had never known love could be this way, and she told him so as she snuggled down against his bare body and hugged him closer.

"I love you, Zackery Elsworth."

"I love you, too. Now, aren't you glad I stole the distributor cap off your car today?"

"Is that what you did!"

"Yeah. I couldn't think of any other way to be with you."

"Had you ever thought about just asking me?"

"Sure, but I figured you would turn me down."

"Well, I wouldn't have."

"I didn't know that. I thought you and Skip had reconciled."

"I wanted you to think that so you wouldn't keep nagging me to get professional help. Honestly, Zackery. You were a real pain in the you-know-what."

He grinned at her affectionately and lovingly patted her. "It nearly tore my heart out to suggest that you go back to Skip, but I wanted you to be happy."

"I know, and I love you all the more for it."

"You'd better love me more and more and more. . . ." They kissed again lingeringly; then one kiss led to another, then another, and then the hunger took over again.

They made love once more, with searing intensity, their love for each other overflowing all boundaries.

Later, as she lay drowsily in his arms, she thought about all the parties they would be required to attend and how proud she would be to be his wife. "Umm, Judge Zackery Elsworth Tremayne and his—" She considered the proper way to announce a judge and his wife. "What's the proper way to say that?"

"Say what?" he asked in a sleepy voice.

"Say that Judge Tremayne and his wife have arrived."

"The Honorable Judge Zackery Tremayne and his old broad are here. I think that's it."

"Zack!" She punched him in the ribs.

"Hey!" He rolled over and trapped her arms above her head and kissed her into quiet submission.

"Are you happy?"

"Very, very happy," she whispered.

"I'll try my best to always keep you that way, Toni," he promised solemnly.

As they became lost in each other's kisses once more, a bright, searing flash of light suddenly streaked across the room. It lit up the room, casting red, rosy shadows across the walls.

"What in the—" Zack's head popped up and he looked around the room expectantly.

"Oh, dear. I think it's back," Toni said in a resigned voice.

And for a change, it had perfect timing! Maybe *now* he would believe her.

Zack glanced down at her blankly. "What is?"

"You know—the thing."

His eyes grew round as saucers—not necessarily the flying kind, but very round and very large nevertheless. "You mean, the thing—"

"Yeah."

"Where?" he asked in hushed expectation. His eyes darted around the room nervously.

"Well, if I were to make a guess, I'd say it's in your backyard again."

"Oh, come on, Toni. It can't be!"

Slipping out of bed, she extended her hand encouragingly. "Come on. Don't be afraid. I don't think they're here to hurt anyone. I think they're just inquisitive."

Hesitantly, Zack let her lead him out of bed, and they both tiptoed over to the window.

An eerie red glow lit up the room as Toni carefully pulled the curtain back to reveal to Zack's stunned eyes a bright object, almost eighty feet in diameter, hovering silently over his backyard.

"My Lord," he murmured reverently, "it's . . . there. . . ."

"I told you so," she whispered smugly, and

breathed a sign of relief that he had seen it this time. Now let him try and call her nuts.

"What's it doing?" he asked in a hushed tone.

"I don't know, but you can bet it's up to something," she whispered over his shoulder.

The saucer looked like the same one that she had seen the second time. It was large and impressive, with flashing lights that had dimmed somewhat as it had descended to earth.

"Do you think anyone else is seeing this?" Zack asked excitedly.

"No, I doubt it," Toni said glumly. "It seems that no one but me in this neighborhood ever does."

While they watched, the bottom hatch opened, and an arm shot out and carefully replaced an object on the grass.

With lightning speed, the arm withdrew, the hatch closed, and the object shot upward, then streaked away in the night.

"How nice," Toni said pleasantly. "Look what they brought back, Zack."

"My barbecue grill," he said lamely.

"Yeah, I guess they didn't like outdoor cooking. See, I told you they were only inquisitive." She let the curtain drop back into place. "Let's go back to bed."

"Toni, I—" He didn't know what to say. He knew it was impossible, yet he had seen it himself. "I feel I owe you an apology," he stammered weakly. She had seen the darned thing after all!

"Oh, darling." She wrapped her arms around his neck lovingly. "You don't owe me anything. Just let this be an important lesson to you. From now on, you'd better believe me when I tell you something. I'm not talking just to hear my brain rattle. Okay?"

He glanced back out the window worriedly. "Okay. But don't you think we'd better tell someone about this?"

"Nah." She took his hand and began to drag him back to bed, where she felt their time would be much better spent. She had been through all of this before and knew what the outcome would be.

"Maybe someday they'll reveal why they're coming here, but trust me, Zack." She held up a warning finger. "No one would ever believe us now."